Jerusalem Stands Alone

Middle East Literature in Translation
Michael Beard and Adnan Haydar, *Series Editors*

Jerusalem Stands Alone

Mahmoud Shukair

Translated from the Arabic by
Nicole Fares

Syracuse University Press

Syracuse University Press
Syracuse, New York 13244-5290

First Edition 2018
18 19 20 21 22 23   6 5 4 3 2 1

Originally published in Arabic as *Al-Quds waḥda-hâ hunâk*
(Beirut: Hachette Antoine, 2010).

∞ The paper used in this publication meets the minimum
requirements of the American National Standard for Information
Sciences—Permanence of Paper for Printed Library Materials,
ANSI Z39.48—1992.

For a listing of books published and distributed by Syracuse
University Press, visit www.SyracuseUniversityPress.syr.edu.

ISBN: 978-0-8156-1103-5 (paperback)
978-0-8156-5446-9 (e-book)

Library of Congress Cataloging-in-Publication Data
Names: Shuqayr, Maḥmūd author. | Fares, Nicole translator.
Title: Jerusalem stands alone / Mahmoud Shukair ; translated from
    the Arabic by Nicole Fares.
Other titles: Quds waḥdahā hunāk. English
Description: First edition. | Syracuse : Syracuse University Press,
    2018. | Series: Middle East literature in translation
Identifiers: LCCN 2018001310 (print) | LCCN 2018005385
    (ebook) | ISBN 9780815654469 (e-book) | ISBN 9780815611035
    (pbk. : alk. paper)
Classification: LCC PJ7862.H854 (ebook) | LCC PJ7862.H854
    Q3713 2018 (print) | DDC 892.7/803—dc23
LC record available at https://lccn.loc.gov/2018001310

Contents

Acknowledgments

A SPECIAL THANKS to my dear friend, Sara Ramey, whose advice and insight has been indispensable to this novel. Thank you for your time and honesty. And to my parents and brother, whose love and support sustained me throughout.

Nicole Fares

Jerusalem Stands Alone

~

A City

IN THE MORNING I walk to the markets surrounded by the city's history, ghostly layers of people from past eras, men of different ages and women of different times. The living women are careful to avoid physical contact, which the overcrowding all but invites. In this city, soldiers are everywhere.

I return from my usual walk to sit in the Damascus Gate Café on the terrace overlooking the market. The waiter is busy serving other customers. Is he the same waiter from before or someone who looks like him? (Stories of doppelgangers are spreading throughout the city.)

I contemplate the yellowing rocks of the Walls of Jerusalem and the windows of the houses spread out before me. Some are closed, others open, and I imagine the stories and secrets hidden within. I drink tea and watch a thin blonde foreigner slowly sipping her coffee, attentively turning the pages of her book while I spread my papers out in front of me. The woman leaves. (Maybe she's from a different time?)

I remain at the café until evening but the windows of the houses refuse to speak.

Another Evening

AT THE LAST MINUTE, the city realizes it's closing time. In his thick-doored fridge, the fishmonger stores what's left of the fish his hands didn't catch. (He buys fish netted in the Jaffa Sea.) He washes his tile floor with soapy water, and the runoff with its residues and odors escapes down the drain.

The city empties. Its merchants close up their shops and rush home, eyes straight ahead, hoping not to see anything unexpected. And from the Damascus Gate to the Lions' Gate, from Herod's Gate to the New Gate, the city passes a sorrowful night. Through its outdoor and indoor markets, only the homeless wind and the echoes of the soldiers' steps are heard.

Neighbors

HER NAME IS SUZANNE. She's a thin blonde from Marseille who rented a room in the Old City, where she shares a bathroom with her neighbors, a bathroom she uses once in the morning and again around midnight.

Her window overlooks a house occupied by five settlers who appear on the porch every morning. She can see the top of the pale yellow wall not far from the house. (Suzanne loved this city from the moment she arrived last year.)

Suzanne bought a small armoire and set it against the wall that divides her room from her neighbors'. The thin wall was raised to create a surplus room and, despite the lack of space, Suzanne likes it here. She listens to the radio in the evening. (She doesn't have a television set, doesn't like television—she says it drains her soul.)

She feels uncomfortable whenever the voices next door invade her room and bought the armoire, thinking it might block noise from coming through the wall, but it barely helps. Some nights, Suzanne hears her neighbor murmuring to her husband, loud one minute and faint the next. This morning, the neighbor uncharacteristically threw her teacup at the wall, unleashing a barrage of insults at her husband for not letting her travel with her neighbors to al-Aghwar and Jericho, to the Sea of Galilee and Bisan.

The Handkerchief

RABAB COMES OVER sometimes to spend half an hour in Suzanne's room, explaining Arabic words Suzanne doesn't understand, and then spend the rest of the time gossiping comfortably without a chaperone. They exchange heartfelt words—Rabab whispers with her eyes glued to the door while Suzanne, though she whispers, doesn't think what she's saying is secret at all.

Rabab asks what she thinks of the city.

"I like it," Suzanne says. Rabab asks her about Marseille. "I like it, too, but I don't like my mom's boyfriend." They laugh.

Before Rabab returns to her room, she gives Suzanne a silk handkerchief with a map of the city embroidered in the center, which Suzanne hugs to her heart. Rabab smiles shyly as she slips out the door.

~

The Girl

ASMAHAN BECOMES FLUSTERED when she goes to the bathroom to wash up. When she takes off her dress, she sees blood on the fabric but calms down when she remembers her mother's detailed explanation of what would happen. "You're about to become an adult," her mother said. This pleases Asmahan; she's excited to experience womanhood.

She opens the door and frantically calls her mother, who holds her daughter and kisses her tenderly, hiding her own fear of what the girl's future might hold. That day, Asmahan becomes a woman (or so she thinks).

Fear

FEAR IS IN THE MARKETS AND STREETS, beneath the entryways and porches. The father fears for his house and shop, convinced of the treachery of the times. The son is scared of failing his exam and of girls rejecting him when it's time to get married because of his slight limp from an old illness. The mother fears for her daughter, who has just developed breasts, and the daughter is scared of the nightmares stalking her sleep. Meanwhile, the grandmother is afraid because she doesn't know how her granddaughter will behave now that she's grown (the grandmother thinks) two demons on her chest.

~

Doors

I WALK HOME, passing through the Jaffa Gate. Soldiers stop me there, helmets on their heads and swords in their hands. They frisk me and ask, "Where are you going?" "Home," I say. Their spectral commander speaks a Romance tongue, so I know they're foreign. He tells me in broken Arabic, "Walk. Go!"

I go, walking to the New Gate, near the park the Israelis built at the foot of the wall. One of the Israeli prostitutes grabs me. "See the green grass there? It's better than any bed," she says. I pull out of her grasp and keep moving toward the New Gate, where Israeli soldiers detain me. They wear bulletproof helmets and hold machine guns, and ask for my ID, reading it carefully. Their commander asks me, "Mi-eyfo ata?" ("Where are you from?") I answer him, and he tells me in broken Arabic, "Walk!"

At the Damascus Gate, I see on the road someone who looks like a beggar, hurrying toward West Jerusalem, occasionally glancing behind him in terror. I grow suspicious but maintain my pace. A group of knights on horseback follows him, wearing helmets from the Ayyubid period, and Yamani swords hang on their waists. They don't stop me as I move past them.

I walk down Nablus Road and unlock the door. Home. In the mirror, I see myself wearing a helmet. I stand there for half an hour.

Affiliation

WHEN I WAS BORN, the war was two years old. I wonder what my life would have been like if I had been born in the time of Tankz al-Nasiri or Saladin the Victorious. I don't recall the defeat of 1967, but I'm living it now, having been born in a neighborhood a few hundred meters away from the wall. A quiet, self-contained neighborhood, like a well-behaved child. My mother said that on my birthday tanks drove down the street and soldiers fired at houses. "All the west-facing glass shattered"—our house had arched rectangular windows—"and we took cover in a room with east-facing windows, that weren't shot out."

I've been writing about this city for twenty years and I see its past mixing with its present. I'm forty and now, you see, the war is forty-two. The city is more ancient than either of us, too many years to count.

Porches

SET CLOSE TOGETHER, front porches in the old neighborhood exchange secrets. Every two or three days, the porches endure clothes hanging on the lines without complaining about the women who laugh spontaneously. They tolerate the women's whispers, which sometimes last forever.

Nor do the porches mind the men smoking hookah or killing time. The porches, weakened by savage riots, only fear they'll collapse when children lean on their low walls.

In careful silence, the porches mull over the appearance this morning of five settlers. They know that, after this, their existence will never be the same.

~

Friday

THE FISHMONGER goes to Friday prayer. He and his wife leave their house and walk, leaving behind their worldly desires. Asmahan, their thirteen-year-old daughter, stays at home with her grandmother and Rabab says she's going to a friend's house to study. Their eldest son left the country two years ago in pursuit of a woman he loved.

They reach the al-Aqsa Mosque Square, remembering their other son, who was arrested here for throwing rocks at soldiers. They haven't been allowed to visit him for two months, as he's in solitary confinement for assaulting a guard.

The fishmonger and his wife part ways. Khadija goes to the corner where women pray; Abd el-Razzaq to the corner where men pray.

Rabab is on her phone all the way to her Tuesday night date with a boy from college.

A Dress

TUESDAY NIGHT to Friday afternoon is a long wait.

Rabab kills the time in several ways. She reads the Shakespeare assigned to her in college, and the Bertrand Russell and T. S. Eliot, too. She visits Suzanne in her room to hang out with her and watches TV (reruns, romance movies, recent music videos, some news channels). She writes down her thoughts and attempts a few poems in her notebook, then helps her mother sweep and prepare dinner, and stands in front of her bedroom window for half an hour meditating, looking out at the houses. (They are unusually close together and have windows of every size.) Before she goes to bed, she models each and every dress she owns. She can't wait to wear her new red dress out.

She dons it Friday afternoon on a trip to a distant grove, thrilled by his endless compliments, both of the dress and the person wearing it.

~

The Doppelgänger

THE STORY of the double reaches Khadija and she
repeats it over and over and over to her neighbors.

The neighbors quake in fear (inside each burns a
secret desire, curiosity shrouded in expectation). They
gather in a small, secluded area of the market by a metal
door and whisper, sharing intimate words. Then they
laugh. An hour later, they return to their homes amazed
by the things that can happen in this city, so remarkably
jumbled.

Like her neighbors, Khadija is sometimes confused by
this story (and sometimes, like her neighbors, flustered).

~

Mirrors

HIS NAME IS YORAM. He's the police captain in charge of maintaining the city's security.

One afternoon, on the way back to his house to retrieve something, it's as if the captain forgets how to walk. Frozen in his steps, he glances over at a commander who looks like him. Not just like him, though: an identical image. He goes into his garden and the double goes with him while there, on neighboring porches, stand three of his female neighbors. The captain opens his front door and his double does the same. He calls out to his wife but gets no response, and then he remembers that she's still at work. (His double also call out, and receives no response.) The commander thinks he's looking at himself in mirrors set up everywhere. There are no mirrors, though, and his shock pierces to the bone.

When he goes into the living room, he finds no one else standing within the cluster of couches.

~

A Promenade

SHE OPENS HER CLOSET and sees her *jilbāb* but doesn't think of wearing it. Instead, she wears her new burgundy dress out, down the wet alley toward the main street, to find him waiting for her in the car his father (a building contractor) bought him. She sits in the passenger seat and looks around to make sure no one saw her. Another couple sits in the backseat. The girl wears a loose dress and crosses her legs. It's the seventh time these four have driven out to the distant grove to take a walk and have a good time. The boy admires her as a breeze flows through her hair. The car the boy's father bought him accelerates without a care.

Five minutes later, Rabab relaxes and starts to talk, and she hasn't stopped talking since.

Long Beards

THEY APPEAR ON THE PORCH each morning: five of them with long beards. Sometimes, other men and women are with them. They stare ominously at the neighboring houses. When night comes, they get angrier and angrier and finally start firing off their guns at the sky. Around the house, they put up a metal fence and bright lights. The gunfire and noise and excitement that follows them frightens Suzanne. Khadija sticks her head out her bedroom window and yells at them, while her husband begs her to lower her voice. "Don't embarrass us. Be a good girl, now. You know you weren't brought up like that!"

After midnight, the neighborhood grows quiet and everyone falls asleep except for one of the long beards. He's uncomfortable sleeping with the blanket over his beard, and he's uncomfortable with his beard over the blanket, so he just spends all night rearranging his beard.

~~

The Beard

ABD EL-RAZZAQ SAYS, "If he spent his time worrying about his beard, we wouldn't have a problem. If this were his only problem, we would've offered him some solutions. If he hadn't killed one of the young men in the neighborhood because he thought he wanted to harm him, we would've said that his beard is his own business and he's free to do with it what he wants.

"See, the question is what really brought him to this neighborhood. Wouldn't it be better for them and us if he takes his beard back to wherever he came from? There he could wash it, clean it, dry it, perfume it, comb it, make sure it's free of lice and bugs. He could take it with him to the temple and on a walk on the beach. He could talk to it, listen to it, ignore it, display it for ridicule, sell it for cheap. He could do whatever he wants with it, even set fire to it."

Waterdrop

THE FAMILY IS SCATTERED. One son is lost, another in prison. One daughter is on a trip with her friends (her parents think she's studying with a friend from college) and hasn't returned home yet.

Khadija reads the Qur'an after Friday prayer while her husband watches the news. Her husband's worried: he calls his wife but she doesn't answer. Asmahan plays on the computer, and in the kitchen there's a leaky faucet. Every minute a waterdrop, too heavy to hold on, makes a faint, monotonous sound as it falls on the metal of the sink—maybe with purpose, maybe to remind the family of something they've forgotten.

~

Fragility

ASMAHAN GETS READY FOR SCHOOL in the morning. Wearing a blue apron and white socks, she puts on her backpack and is off, cheeks flushed and hair braided. She walks out the door and through the metal fence the settlers erected days ago, pressing against the wall of a house so she can pass through the alley. With some difficulty, she catches up to the girls waiting for her.

Together they walk to school, gliding over the tiles of the market street like a flock of pigeons, and chatter about schoolwork and exams (they're all afraid of their math teacher). They talk about their dreams; some are happy and others aren't. Asmahan complains about the pain the settlers are causing her family. Suddenly, she stops talking and apologizes to her friends for ruining their fragile morning.

~

Phone Call

YORAM CALLS HIS WIFE. He tells her that he's coming home at eleven that night. She says, "Five minutes ago, you said you were coming back at ten." He's surprised because he didn't call her five minutes ago. She received a call from him, she assures him, and told him she'd wait for his return.

Yoram grows suspicious. He's sure his double is playing tricks on him again. He calls in his usual troop of men and sets up an ambush around his house that lasts until one in the morning. Then he goes inside and falls asleep in his wife's arms, but for some reason, she can't sleep.

~

Hymns

THEY COME FROM THE SETTLEMENTS inside the wall and sit in the indoor market, wearing small black hats and chanting parts of hymns before they fall silent. Their diet is dry bread.

The air of the market is humid as one of them scratches his beard, carefully examining it while the owner of the Maqsadi Restaurant sits a few feet away. His restaurant is empty (it's neither lunchtime nor dinnertime), though the smell of falafel suffuses the air. The owner worries that his restaurant will be seized or shut down.

They sit on chairs and their hymns reverberate in the sultry air. Suzanne shows up with a book in her hand and stands nearby, listening to them sing, their long, heavy beards resting on their chests, before she goes inside the restaurant, descends five stairs, and sits at a table close to the entrance. The waiter brings her falafel pieces and a plate of hummus. She eats slowly, skimming her book.

She leaves the restaurant half an hour later but the hymns continue until ten at night. That evening, the restaurant owner gets no rest, but the man who is always preoccupied with his beard does. Tonight, he is exhausted. He tucks his beard under the covers and falls asleep.

If Only

IF ONLY HE KNEW where he was right now. If only he knew his phone number or mailbox number. If only he knew what city he lived in. If only he knew, he would have called him. He would have asked him to come home. He would have told him about Suzanne, who is renting one of the rooms in the house. He would have told him about her beauty and manners and how much this girl loves Palestinians. He would've talked to him as he talks to a friend. "Look, if you like foreign women so much, then come home and meet this girl. Who knows? She might give you her heart and be your support through all the dark times of this treacherous life."

If only he knew where he was . . .

~~

Coffee Cups

THERE ARE FIVE OF THEM. They come out on the porch carrying automatic weapons, gazing at the neighboring houses with eyes shrouded in darkness and secrecy. They sit in bamboo chairs on the porch and lean their guns against the wall. Silently, they drink their coffee, their eyes alone still speaking, while houses cast vast, cool shadows over the alleys and streets. The men don't care. They don't care about the peace of this lovely morning, they just swallow their coffee, grab their guns, and leave, empty coffee cups abandoned on the porch.

They reappear on the porch in the evening, beards dirty and unruly. The five abandoned coffee cups shiver in the cold (or, perhaps, in the expectation that strange things will soon come to pass).

Puzzled

KHADIJA FEELS PUZZLED AND AWKWARD. She hears footsteps coming up the stairs before the door opens and her husband walks in, earlier than usual. She isn't sure whether the man is her husband or his double. He walks up to her as he always does, comfortably, with no intent to dominate or intimidate, but she looks at him in surprise. He looks back at her and asks tenderly, "What is it, woman?"

Khadija studies him suspiciously. Her stare wakes something inside him and he tells her, "Come, Khadija, come," taking hold of her hand to lead her into the bedroom. She grows more suspicious. Should she kick him out? Should she ask him to prove that he's really her husband?

He says, "Your look stirs something deep inside me." She says, "Why did you come home early?" He says he felt tired and came home to rest, then pulls her onto the bed, explaining that rest is only pleasant after hard work.

Khadija dispels the doubts from her mind, but the incident lodges in her memory for days and then weeks.

The Search

IN YORAM'S ATTEMPT to understand everything about the city, he reads a secret log dating back to 1817. The log inventories munitions the Ottomans hid in the Tower of David: 121 barrels of gunpowder (and then another 18.5), 130 crates of lead bullets, and 2,500 cannonballs (some large but most small). The Ottoman commander, Ahmad Agha al-Qutub of Jerusalem, took it upon himself to hide away these munitions for a time of great need.

Yoram sends his men to the tower to look for the munitions but they find nothing, so he summons the descendants of Ahmad Agha for questioning, hoping that one of them will know the whereabouts of the arsenal.

Yoram gets nothing out of them but swears he will not rest until he figures out where those munitions are.

Warmth

RAIN OUTSIDE, warmth in the bed—the troubles of life are held at bay for now. She loves the fading light at this hour. Maybe that's the best someone of forty-five can hope for. (He always assures her that she still looks twenty-five.) She lifts the wool covers and sniffs his chest, saying, "You smell fishy, like you haven't had a shower this evening." He sniffs her chest and tells her, "The fish smell coming from you is enough for the both of us." She likes that, so she sidles closer to him and gives in to the sound of long-awaited rain as it soaks the streets of the neighborhood.

~

Washing

A LIGHT DRIZZLE falls over the city and washes the
alleys, the markets, and the roofs. It washes the old stones
and familiar marble, plays with clotheslines and caresses
windowpanes.

Standing by her bedroom window, Suzanne watches
the city bathing unselfconsciously and remembers the
rain in another city. Overcome with forgotten feelings,
she gets the urge to take a shower and goes to the bathroom she shares with her neighbors, where she spends
half an hour clashing with the water.

Smooth Leg

I'M IN THE CAFÉ, as usual.

The wall and market face me, the entrance to the mosque on my left, the road leading up to the old neighborhood on my right. The stones recall a departed world.

At the mosque entrance, soldiers monitor the market crowd. Prolonged calls to prayer sound, cheap wares are sold, and women haggle with merchants.

In the café is the thin blonde foreigner, one leg stretched comfortably beneath the table as if she were at home. The smooth leg rests in her friend's lap and he strokes it as if it were his cat. The owner of the restaurant approaches them, places two cups of coffee on the table, and retreats.

The soldiers don't retreat. The worshippers enter and exit the mosque and the woman keeps her leg on her friend's lap until sundown, while I study everything around me as though it were my first time here, unsure of what to say, and the café looks confused.

～

Violation

THE CITY GATES are unlocked night and day. In the past, the gates would have been fastened by sundown for fear of a sudden raid. Back then, people inside the wall slept in fragile tranquility. (Once, foreign soldiers opened a hole in the wall, broke into the city, and killed many people.)

Now the city is empty. What good are locked gates?

The fishmonger fidgets in his chair and wonders: when will the violation of the city cease? He doesn't like the current situation. He curses and falls silent again.

Antiques

I SIT IN MY FRIEND'S STORE, which is packed with Eastern antiques he sells to tourists along with miniatures of mosques and churches, rosaries, some made of beads and others of shells, kaffiyehs and shirts emblazoned with religious pieties, woodcarvings, and porcelain and copper versions of city sights. I sit there and watch—the passersby, the wet market, crowded with buildings, the city radiant and women strolling its markets, some to shop and others to distract themselves from the pressures of life.

Worshippers walk down the Via Dolorosa, following a group of people carrying incense and musical instruments while chanting mournful hymns. I listen to the chants and music incrementally filling the market air. I feel the city slip into a state of numbness and drowsiness, and then I spot her at the back of the procession. My friend, surprised to see me stand up to leave, asks me where I'm going, but I only mumble unintelligibly.

I approach the procession determined to show her what has been weighing on me for years. I search and search but can't find her.

∽

Predictions

HE SAYS, "We watched our kid grow up before our eyes. He's our eldest. His mother breastfed him when he was hungry and I bought him the finest clothes in the market.

"He grew to be a tall young man, with a beard and moustache. He makes a lasting impression on girls and any of them would love to have him as her husband. His mother and I witnessed his every step and always reminded him of our love for him. He was the finest human specimen.

"Except our beloved son is gone. A foreigner stole his heart and then flew away without him, leaving him to roam the world in search of her. I suspect he hasn't stopped searching.

"His mother and I are left to sit here on our porch, and console each other from time to time with optimistic stories of the future."

~

Invisible

HE SAYS, "I stare at them standing on the porch facing ours, and they don't look my way, don't look me in the eyes. They behave as though I'm not there. They look only at the house and examine its stones, windows, and the roof we use for airing the laundry and sometimes for sunbathing. They examine everything that has to do with the house, though I tell them, 'Look at me. Look into my eyes.' But they pay me no heed, as if I am invisible.

"They look at the house like it's the only thing they see. I scream at them, 'I belong here! You don't belong here!' But they pay no mind to me. One of them stops looking at the house and stares down at his beard, examining it as if it were the first time he has seen it."

College Girl

SHE'S PROUD to have a girl in college. Here, she lives her life one accomplishment after another, speaking to her neighbors of her daughter's studies in English literature, and her Shakespeare plays. The neighbors find nothing special in what she's telling them because they have sons and daughters in college, too.

She would've spoken of Rabab and her college for just five minutes if one of the neighbors hadn't pointed out that Shakespeare had Arabic roots. His real name, in fact: Sheikh Zbeer. Khadija is skeptical and says her daughter never mentioned that during any of their conversations.

This discussion lasts hardly two minutes but it's brought up again and expanded upon afterward whenever the neighbors meet.

∾

Thorns

WHEN MY WORDS don't obey me, I am in pain. I age a year or two in one day.

When my words refuse to leave me, I feel empty. When they patronize me, I feel ashamed and fragile. I look for an exit but can't decide on one.

When I can't think of a single word that feels sweet to my tortured heart, my nights grow long and I lie on a bed of thorns where shadowless words carry no rhythm. I become suspended outside myself in a dark, abandoned well into which no words have rained in over a hundred years.

A Mirror

IN FRONT OF THE MIRROR by her bed, she dresses very conservatively before leaving the house with her oldest daughter. Her other daughter is with them, too, and she is starting to develop breasts.

Rabab goes with her mother to her friend's wedding. She flicks her head upward like a horse whenever they pass a group of guys, as Asmahan runs in circles around her mother. The mother walks with a dignified air, chest overflowing with desires mingling enjoyment, disappointments, and warnings. The singing alone reverberates in the atmosphere.

She crosses the court, self-conscious of where the café owner and her husband, the fishmonger, sit with the other neighborhood men who are wearied of harsh days. But their eyes contain a glow that cannot be hidden from her. She will let go of her reservations soon enough and throw herself into dancing, which will take her back twenty years.

∽

Dancing

THE GUYS GATHER NEARBY, dressed in their usual jeans and short-sleeve shirts because girls like a rugged look. They hear the women singing in the distance and can't control themselves much longer. They try to concentrate on dancing to the music played by an amateur band but each boy has a girl on his mind.

They don't return home until the band stops playing and they've unwound.

~

Sweat

THE NEIGHBORHOOD GIRLS won't let the night pass without making an impression. They show off their dancing skills to attract the attention of mothers scouting for brides for their sons. They sway to the rhythm of the radio or live music. And they don't leave the dance floor until they're sweating, having somewhat soothed their desires and glimpsed a hopeful future.

Mingling

THE LITTLE GIRLS stand in line beside their mothers. They dance randomly and then rush outside to play and run around, but the mothers pay them no mind. They're occupied with the dancing, which mingles memories and a trace of sorrow because what has passed will never return. There's no time to remember the loved ones who are no longer. Here, sorrow is forever postponed.

The mothers return to their neighborhood and its secrets that they know so well, aware they are no longer what they were earlier that evening.

Calf

SHE LOOKS CONFUSED for some reason. The curtains are closed and her life seems a mystery, fragments of experience crowding her mind, some hers, others she's read about in books or heard about from chatty women.

And he's strutting in front of her in a black suit, hair sticking up like a coxcomb. Her hair rests on her shoulders and she wears a flowing white dress like a thin summer cloud that could float away at any moment. This entire setting implies a particular intent.

He appreciates her unprecedented nervousness, touches her right leg to comfort her, brushes her calf with calculated affection.

She asks him to open the window, buying herself time before the inevitable collision.

Rhythm

THE NEIGHBORHOOD SLEEPS in a rhythm fraught with visions near and far, weaving recent moments with those a thousand years past.

In this night flow images of rivers and spacious fields of wheat and barley and corn, and of river mouths and innumerable animals, and of a burning passion that dies only to be reignited with new intensity.

~

Porch

SHE PERCHES on the bamboo chair in her nightgown, and though the humid morning has passed, she remains seated with her legs crossed. On the neighbor's porch, she sees only laundry.

The laundry hangs on clotheslines, whispering. She listens carefully but can't understand what's being said. She thinks the laundry must be muttering of all the fun nights that will come to an end.

She stretches her arms like a bird preparing to fly, then brings them back to her side, her hands in her lap, as if she regrets having made a movement that cost her great effort.

Her clothes, which she has worn all week, lie on the kitchen floor, in the bedroom corner, by the closet, and under the bed. These clothes miss the line. She said that she would put them in the washing machine this morning but morning came and went, and she enjoys gazing at the wall peeking from behind the buildings while the clothesline grows tired of waiting.

∾

A Lack

I LOOK UP from my papers to find that the foreign woman left when I wasn't looking. The café feels empty now. The owner brings me a cup of coffee—my seventh today—and I take a sip, admiring the shaded rooftops of houses that pay me no heed, busy with private affairs they don't wish to disclose. My mind is torn between my papers and these houses.

Questions multiply, pricking my mind like thorns.

Ascent

ON MY WAY TO LIONS' GATE, I see him staggering uphill, bearing his cross toward the city that will never forget him. He stops to rest when he's too tired, then walks forward again to his fate. The good-hearted poor surround him, wrapped in sorrow and silence as the army stands watch over the scene until the end.

He walks the rough road bearing that cross. Beside the path, a mother grieves while the city stands oblivious to the tragedy unfolding in its streets. He faces his fate without blaming the city, while the city pays no attention to the flowing blood.

It will wake up soon, though, as if shaken by an earthquake.

༄

A Passing

AS I AMBLE through the city streets, I think of paying
Sufyan a visit in his store on Via Dolorosa. He tells me,
"You've come at the perfect time," without explaining
why. Minutes later, I see her walking by the store, tall,
hair in two braids. She slows down and glances toward
Sufyan, then walks away. He tells me on his way out,
"Stay here, I won't be long."

I remain in the store looking out at the street, watching people, expecting someone to walk in—maybe a
tourist looking to buy an antique—but twenty minutes
pass and no one enters. My attention switches to the daily
newspaper and obituaries.

Fifty minutes pass and Sufyan has not returned. A
tourist and her friend walk into the store and look around
for ten minutes. The girl buys a kaffiyeh and the guy buys
prayer beads strung beside a square block engraved with
a picture of the Church of the Holy Sepulchre. They pay
and leave, and I place the money in the drawer. Then I
sit back down and wait, but no other customers walk in.

Two hours later, Sufyan is back. I'm angry at him for
having confined me to his store all this time but he only
laughs playfully as I leave, suffused with rage.

Knights

YORAM GOES OUT AT NIGHT in disguise to inspect the city's defenses. He roams the streets as a beggar (inspired by the undercover Israeli police) and heads toward the Damascus Gate. There are just a few men and three Israeli streetwalkers on the route leading from the New Gate to the Damascus Gate.

As he approaches the gate, he sees a brigade of horsemen. At first, he thinks they're his unit and approaches them confidently, but as he nears, he sees that these horsemen wear an unfamiliar uniform and helmets that date as far back as the Ayyubid era, with Yamani swords hanging at their sides.

Yoram becomes flustered, but luckily he's disguised—one of the horsemen might've stabbed him.

He turns on his heels and hurries back to headquarters to order his men to take out the horsemen, but though the police forces mobilize and search until morning for the knights, they can't find anyone who fits the description.

Yoram is convinced the brigade is hiding somewhere, and he will arrest them one night.

~

In Hiding

GHAZAL (his nickname was bestowed by a man fond of irony) is the administrative manager at a city hospital. He still remembers that afternoon when people protested on the streets. His friend, the male nurse, had just finished sedating a woman in her thirties who was laid out on the bed, all made up, with the administrative manager monitoring the anaesthetization (he wouldn't have had to observe if this were a better hospital). Then they heard gunshots. Soldiers opened fire at the protesters and the doctor and nurses ran out to the porch to watch.

Ghazal remained in the operating room alone. He approached the woman's body and inhaled every inch of it. He pushed the thin white robe open and was admiring her beautiful full breasts when a bullet ricocheted off the window of the operating room. He ducked under the bed and remained there until minutes before the operation.

Sufyan

HE'S A STRANGE MAN. He doesn't leave the city, remaining tucked inside its walls. He spends his time in the bar, as if he and the bar were conjoined twins. He's single and is not interested in marriage, drinking wine from dawn to dusk, taking a big gulp from his glass every few minutes. Life seems sweet to him sometimes—at other times, bitter.

He guffaws as if exhaling bottled-up wrath and mourns the city he refuses to leave. His face is a heated stove as he reaches for the wineglass he keeps hidden from customers, while he keeps his eyes on the road as if waiting for a date.

He exits the bar, leaving everything behind him, and doesn't return for a while. Then he comes back, inevitably drawn back to this city he can never leave, as if he and the city are conjoined twins.

A Lilac Robe

ASMAHAN'S VOICE COMES TO HIM, calling his name. She asks him to fetch her lilac robe. (She's been cranky lately because she can't sit out on the porch anymore.) She tells him she forgot to bring it into the bathroom with her.

He looks for her lilac robe and finds it in the wardrobe. She says the bathroom door is unlocked, so he presses down the handle and opens the door.

He's struck by her nudity. She glances over at him drowsily as she turns off the water, and a nervous smile makes its way to her lips as if it's the first time he's seen her naked. As she dries herself, he thinks to himself that she could've wrapped herself with the blue towel and left instead. But he likes this behavior of hers, a mixture of boldness and shyness.

Before he drapes the robe over her full figure, Asmahan stands in front of the bathroom door rubbing her eyes. The scene that began comfortably ends awkwardly, with whispered apologies.

꽁

A Memory

HE TELLS HER, as she presses her right foot in between his feet, that one afternoon his mother went into the bathroom with a bucket to shower. The water was off that day and the faucet wouldn't release a single drop. His mother forgot to take a cup to scoop water from the bucket, and she called for him to bring her one.

The bathroom lock was broken, so she couldn't secure it from the inside. He opened the door. He was twelve at the time and kept his eyes glued to the ceiling as he moved closer to his mother, but as he turned to leave, his eyes glided over her enigmatic pale figure. He walked out and reprimanded himself for not having closed his eyes.

The pressure from her right foot stops and, heavy with exhaustion, she closes her eyes, while his sleep is intermittent and remains so until morning.

The Helmet

I'M WALKING THROUGH THE BAZAAR, heading to-ward Jaffa Gate from the side of Suwayq Alley, when I see him riding a white mare toward the vast field, sur-rounded by a formation of horsemen. It's evening, and the market is swamped with men and women of different nationalities. I see the king in his steel helmet, looking in every direction.

The merchants stand outside their shops and watch the scene unfold. One of the tourists asks me, "What era are we in?" I tell him, "We're in the foreign era, and what you're seeing here is one of the kings who once ruled Jerusalem." I ask one of the merchants (originally from Venice, he came to Jerusalem with one of the foreign crusades), "Do you sell helmets like the king's? I want one as a souvenir."

He says, "We're fresh out of helmets. Come back in a week—we're getting a large shipment from Florence."

I forget the exact date, but I return after a while and can't find the merchant, or his shop, or the king and his knights. Only the city remains.

Between Two Scenes

SUZANNE ENTERS THE TREE-COVERED VALLEY. Looking around, she sees the Church of All Nations nearby, and her mind travels back to the ancient past as she watches him fashion his cross from tree limbs. He bows, afraid of death for the first time. She shivers and wishes she'd brought her friend, whose presence might have made this moment less painful, if only slightly.

She remains among the trees for some time, ignoring the traffic noise coming from a nearby street and another strange humming sound. She sees him trudging along, so she paces beside him, listening to the people whimper and sigh. She walks the Via Dolorosa from beginning to end before reaching the Church of the Holy Sepulchre and sitting on the steps facing the church gate. (If only she'd brought her friend!) The ancient scene plays out before her in its entirety. She sees the masses gather around him and weep. She sees the present-day scene and weeps, her mind caught between the two.

～

Something

ASMAHAN RETURNS FROM SCHOOL with her class-
mate Mary and their girlfriends. As they stroll through
the streets, the girls add to the city a glow they're too
young to recognize. Sufyan is aware of it, however, as
he sits in his shop waiting for tourists to buy his wooden
sculptures, his photographs of the city, his crucifixes and
other religious relics.

Asmahan bids Mary good-bye and walks down the
empty alley to her house. Mary turns onto another
empty alley leading to her own home. Sufyan feels lonely.
He gulps his wine then closes his shop early to walk the
market streets anxiously, as if looking for something, and
the scents of the city trigger old memories.

Running

I RECALL HODJA BITTERLY. He walked by a crowd of little girls and boys playing in the city square who gathered around him to hear a story. He shooed them away but they refused to leave.

He thought of a way to get the kids to leave him be, so he glanced up toward the nearby neighborhood and said, "Look, there's a wedding over there! What are you all still doing here?" The kids believed his lie and ran in the direction he was pointing.

When he saw them running enthusiastically, he thought to himself, *It looks like there really is a wedding*!

And he ran after the little boys and girls, and I ran with him. I ran for a different reason—a reason that was not funny at all.

A Boy and a Girl

THE CITY KEEPS BUSY and I keep busy with everything
I lay my eyes on—a girl wriggling out of her mother's
grip at the market, her mother running after her as she
laughs carelessly. I grow bored sitting at my uncle's store
waiting for my father and fall asleep until the girl comes
in and sits beside me, her dress bunching up around her
knees as she sits down. She caresses my hair tenderly. I
reach out and on a whim pull her dress down but she
grabs my hand and says, "Come." I stand up and follow
her. She runs and I run after her, then next to her, and we
don't come back until nightfall.

I open my eyes and see people I don't recognize. The
city keeps itself busy and I'm a few years older. I wish I
could see the girl in front of me as I did in the dream—I
wish she could really come to me, with that innocence,
in that dress.

∽

One Afternoon

THE CITY KEEPS BUSY and I follow the girl to the end of the marketplace. She takes an alley to her house and goes inside while I stop and wait. Her blue school uniform and white socks mesmerize me. Her hair is dark auburn, her eyes hazel, and she laughs with her schoolmates. When they separate, she invariably hurries home looking straight ahead while I stick behind her like her shadow, too shy to speak. She is too, apparently.

But she's hypnotized my senses. Every afternoon as my body sits in the classroom, my mind and soul are here, on the road where my fifteen-year-old beloved walks.

I wait for her one afternoon to get out of school but she doesn't emerge. I wait for her the next day, I wait days and weeks, but still she doesn't show. That was last fall. I frequent the road she walked on, trying to track her by smell, like her pet dog.

Sky Blue

ABD EL-RAZZAQ brings three men with him. They work on the house for three days, painting it luminous sky blue. They paint all the rooms, including Suzanne's. They paint the front door and the staircase and the storage room where they keep the furniture. Abd el-Razzaq says he likes the color. Khadija says she likes it, too. In fact, she was the one who suggested the color in the first place and her husband agreed instantly.

The house looks its best tonight. Khadija struts around its rooms in a light blue dress, feeling one with the house.

Saturday

IT'S SATURDAY, and heavy rain pools in the markets and flows in shallow rivers. The shop owners stay inside, cold, waiting for customers, but the rain has trapped people in their homes.

And the Orthodox Jews, with their long beards and black coats, pass through the Gate of the Valley to the synagogue despite the rain.

Asmahan tells her friend Mary as they look out the classroom window, "I wish the teacher would let us go outside to play in the rain." Mary says, "We can when school is out."

This Saturday stands apart from other days because it's stopped raining by the time Asmahan and Mary get out of school. There are only scattered puddles that make it difficult to walk through the market.

~

The Grandmother

RABAB SAYS: "My grandmother died on a very cold and rainy day. We carried her out of our house to al-Aqsa Mosque to pray over her body and then to Via Dolorosa. We walked past the Lions' Gate and went left toward the cemetery. Grandma's funeral wasn't a big one because of the weather, and anyway, Grandma wouldn't have wanted a big funeral. That's what she used to tell us.

"We buried her by my grandfather's grave. He died fifteen years before she did and Grandma used to talk about him all the time. She spoke constantly of him until the day she died." Gesturing toward the sky, Rabab continues, "She used to say that she was waiting for the moment when she could be reunited with him.

"And then the moment came, and Grandma left Jerusalem that afternoon to reunite with him."

∽

The Young Son

HE SAYS, "Our young son, Abd el-Rahman, was released from jail and came home. His mother and two sisters were very happy, and I was happy for his return. His mother stood at the porch of our house and ululated again and again while the settlers stood on the neighboring porch and watched us uneasily.

"Our son, Abd el-Rahman, got out of jail with a long and unruly beard. I felt bad for him because he suffers from an old illness. I secretly prayed that God bring an end to these dark days. I hate bigotry and bigots (Farid al-Din Attar considered bigotry to be ignorance). His mother raised a white flag on our rooftop in celebration of the return of our imprisoned son.

"The men and women from our neighborhood all came to congratulate us. His mother danced like a young woman, and his two sisters danced, and Suzanne danced too. All the women danced and sang until midnight.

"In the stillness of the night, Abd el-Rahman cried as he begged God for forgiveness. But he wouldn't say why he was crying. I raised my hand to my heart and prayed aloud for God to bring an end to these dark days."

~

Residency

SUZANNE SAYS that she'll only marry a man after careful scrutiny. Her father separated from her mother a few years earlier and that left a painful mark on her. She stayed with her mother until she was twenty while her father lived with another woman. She says, "When Mom found out that dad had a mistress, she hit her head against the wall every morning. She turned Dad's mornings so bitter, he would jump out of bed, put on his pants, and run out of the house without coffee or breakfast.

"Then Mom started dating a guy who looked like he played the villain in a horror movie. His stares used to scare me whenever he visited. I moved out and spent three years migrating from place to place before I moved here to Jerusalem, and the moment I arrived, I said to myself that I'd stay here forever if I could."

Loss

I WALK through the alleys of the city, looking at the high windows, seductively arched windows that cry out for admiration. I wait, hoping she'll look out one of the windows and my happiness will return to me after so long.

I look and I search, I search and I look, and my search takes a long time. Then I see a girl who looks like her—I think maybe it is she, but she looks different after so long.

I wave at her to open her window and come down to the alleyway. She disappears behind the window with flowers and flowerpots on its ledge.

I wait, and the wait consumes me.

Reassurance

ABD EL-RAZZAQ and Khadija are worried for their child, whose head is being X-rayed. She sits a while in the waiting room, then stands up and paces anxiously. Abd el-Razzaq stands up and sits down whenever Khadija does. The doctor comes out and says the results of the X-ray are satisfactory and that the girl's condition is nothing to worry about.

Abd el-Razzaq and Khadija are happy. Khadija regains her energy as if she has just been pulled from a deep well, pushing her chest forward proudly. He avoids eyeing her breasts so as not to provoke gossip. Taking hold of her hand, he leads her down the hallways to check on their daughter behind the glass. Uncharacteristically, she allows him to lead her.

~

Meeting

HER NAME IS HALA.

I see her walking in the market, taking fragile steps. When I greet her, she asks me who I am, and we walk together once I've introduced myself. The market smells fresh from an earlier rain.

She speaks to me of the Katamon neighborhood, of her youth, of the pillaged houses. Then she looks into my eyes and says, "But who are you?" I answer her, then express my admiration of what her father wrote all those years ago about his wife's breathtaking beauty, and his grief over losing the mother of his children, and about him raising his two daughters and a son after her death.

When she's reassured, we resume walking in the market's eerie air. She says she's very tired. I warn her to be careful not to slip and suggest we drink a glass of orange juice at the neighboring diner.

We settle in the diner like two old friends. I listen to her recount bits of her stories, while outside, rain patters on the city streets, on the diner, on Aftimos Road, and on the Lutheran Church of the Redeemer.

She goes silent before saying that the rain transports her to that distant fall.

Wailing

HER NAME IS BARBIE.

She read her father's manuscript in Beirut as I cried in Jerusalem. I cried in bed while Mother moved between my bed and the broken window. Barbie didn't know me and I didn't know her, but she claims she heard a child cry that night.

She says her heart was dislodged, that her breasts went numb, swelled, and filled with milk.

On our way to a restaurant nearby, I tell her, "I wish I had known." She says, "How could you have? You were a child at the time who only knew how to cry." We laugh together. It's evening. Barbie tells me about her mother, who died before reaching fifty. About her brother, who died young. About her father, who died of sorrow. About the house her father built from his sweat and blood.

The restaurant in Zahra Street is empty as I pull a heavy leather chair out for her and ask her to have a seat.

Barbie and I sit down, and we can hear wailing.

The House

WE VISIT THE HOUSE TOGETHER.

Barbie says, "Let's go before the sun begins to set," so we take the bus to Katamon and the other passengers ignore us. Instead, they pretend that we don't exist—we, the natives who should hurry up and go extinct so they can enjoy this country. We get off at the end of the street and walk a little.

She says, "How I walked in this neighborhood. How I played. How I danced!" And I follow her as she puts together the pieces of her long story.

When we reach the house, a woman on the porch asks us, "Ma ata rotse?" (What do you want?)

Barbie says, "I want to see the house."

I interject, "Many Palestinians have been coming back these past years to see their houses," and add, "Edward Said has!"

A frowning man steps out on the porch and a young girl, probably his daughter, steps from behind him. I say, "This tragedy has lasted long enough. You can't keep ignoring it." Barbie then says, "I want to see my bedroom." The man tells her to go to the Israeli housing authority, that maybe she'll find her bedroom there. The woman adds, "Yes, leave, we have nothing to do with you."

The young girl watches, bewildered, like she had no idea what's going on. And Barbie, who doesn't get to see her bedroom, turns around and walks away as I follow behind.

And the house remains standing, silent.

Crawl

HE SAYS, "I saw them early one morning, scoping out the side of the house. They marked the walls with red ink and then went on gently caressing their long beards. I told them to get away from our house, and one of them said, 'This is our house and we have the papers to prove it.' I told them that their papers were forged.

"They just went back on marking the walls.

"The people gathered. Journalists, photographers, news stations. Khadija and I were in the middle of the crowd. What was happening upset Abd el-Rahman. Rabab and Asmahan stood, paralyzed with fear, and Suzanne stood right there next to us in disbelief.

"The soldiers arrived and ordered people to disperse. My wife and I climbed the stairs to the house and stood silently behind the window.

"Abd el-Rahman sat in his room reading the Quran while Suzanne went off to her job. The soldiers stood in front of our house until evening, rooted there like old trees."

Laundry

SUZANNE BOUGHT a small washing machine some days earlier. She sets her laundry on a cycle and goes to work and in the evening she, unlike the rest of the women in the neighborhood, takes her laundry up to the roof of the house. She finds Abd el-Rahman walking up there, prayer beads in hand. (Abd el-Rahman says that evil surrounds us.) Suzanne doesn't speak to him so as not to add to his stress and he doesn't speak to her in the name of chastity and controlling his lust. She compares him to his brother, who is traveling the world in search of the woman he loves, and ponders how people choose such different paths.

She hangs her laundry on the clothesline and wonders how far her relationship will go with her boyfriend, who is interning at a law office. He hasn't proposed to her but if he does, she will say yes. He hinted at it some days ago when he said, "This city is overpopulated. Where would people live if they wanted to get married?"

Suzanne finishes hanging her clothes and admires the rooftops of the neighboring houses, not paying any attention to Abd el-Rahman. She glances at the occupied houses. They're strangely silent, though she sees a few people on this or that roof. She feels a familiarity with this city, resting beneath the blanket of night.

Half an hour later, she's back home. She takes off her dress, embroidered in red and green, lies still in bed, and touches her young body for a second. She tries to gather her scattered thoughts and center herself. Three hours later, she falls asleep, having arranged only a few of them.

~

Mood

RABAB WASHES HER JEANS, dresses, shirts, and underwear by hand. She believes washing machines destroy clothes. Fortunately for the washing machine companies, Rabab has only shared her theory with a few people. She did try to talk Suzanne out of buying a washing machine but Suzanne wasn't convinced.

Rabab enjoys hand-washing her clothes, attentively scrubbing them in water and soap. She takes her time, the clothes playing back and forth in her hands. Washing her clothes and hanging them out in the sun once a week, and every day during her period, rejuvenates her.

For a time, she feels warm, awash in affection for her body and clothes.

The Thin Blonde

I SIT IN A CAFÉ. The weather is moderate and the evening city markets are nearly vacant. I drink my coffee. My mind is scattered.

I see the thin foreign blonde darting through the market. (I asked the café owner what her name is: Suzanne.) I think, "Maybe something happened to Suzanne." I ruminate on her for some time and write down on paper discordant sentences as Suzanne departs and then appears, appears then departs, until suddenly, I stand and follow her. I look for her in the alleys and markets, and I don't find her.

~

Her and the House

SINCE KHADIJA GOT MARRIED, she's been away from the house a handful of times. Abd el-Razzaq was in too much of a rush to wait for summer, so they had an unusual winter wedding. He took her to Jericho for their honeymoon and rented a furnished apartment for a month.

On only one other occasion has she been out of the house: when she had to stay in the hospital for ten days. How she missed him then. Every day she asked Abd el-Razzaq, "When can I come home?"

Afterward she returned home, and other than on these occasions, she cannot remember being away for more than a day or two.

She tells her neighbors, "I came into this house on my wedding day, and I will leave it on the day I die."

∽

Confusion

ABD EL-RAHMAN remembers them now. He remembers the cells and the rooms at the police station where he spent long, weary months.

He remembers them all: the fanatics, the moderates, the secularists, the others in between. Each tried to lure him to their side but Abd el-Rahman did not take sides. He did, however, pick up some of their philosophies. They steeped in his mind, a wondrous brew of ideas, and now, out of jail, he sees evil everywhere. There must be absolution.

He is uncertain of the things he says at times, unsure of this road to absolution. He cries, and a wave of uncertainty floods him.

～

An Hour Later

I GO BACK TO THE HOUSE, soon to be evacuated, to write an article about it in the newspaper. The owner, Abd el-Razzaq, welcomes me, and, though I am a stranger, the females of the house do not veil themselves in my presence. Khadija, his wife, immediately offers me coffee. His oldest daughter, Rabab, brings me a plate of fruit. His youngest, Asmahan, stands at the door with a book in her hand. Later I'm told that the eldest son, Marwan, is drifting about somewhere in the world. Abd el-Rahman is out, but if he had been at home he would have complained about his mother and sisters appearing unveiled in front of a stranger.

It's evening and raining outside, overcast weather that inspires me to write. Abd el-Razzaq busily recounts the facts as I jot down notes and look up every now and then. Khadija, sitting by her husband, frequently fills in the information missing from his narration. I glance at Rabab, who sits listening, and our eyes meet. Her doe eyes are honey colored. Asmahan sits in the far corner with a book in her hand.

After an hour of taking notes, I become less interested in the soon-to-be evacuated house and more interested in Rabab.

Her Firstborn

KHADIJA SAYS that she gave birth to her eldest son in her bedroom. She went into labor sometime past midnight. It wasn't possible to take her to the hospital because the army blocked the streets and roads.

Abd el-Razzaq told her, "You will have to put up with the pain until morning comes."

For two hours she tolerated the pain.

Abd el-Razzaq's mother brought a bowl of hot water, a towel, and some cloths. As a young girl, she'd watched many midwives deliver babies. Sitting between Khadija's legs, she prayed to God to keep evil at bay. Half an hour later, Marwan showed his head and began to cry. The windows of the house were tightly shut. Outside, rain poured and curfew was in effect.

~

Grass

HANAN IS CAUGHT IN GHAZAL'S WEB. They first met when he solicited the architecture firm where she works. After that, he made a habit of stopping by her office when her boss was out. Pulling her to his chest, he'd lift her dress.

She didn't stop him. She did ask him to make things between them halal, but he has a way of not promising anything while still making her feel he's not refusing her request.

Two days after she's fired from work, he takes her in the evening to a mountain crowded with trees. He tells her, "Lie down with me on the grass and close your eyes," so she does. A moment later, he hears a scratching noise from the forest. Terrified, he takes off running.

Hanan lies with her eyes closed for five more minutes. Then she gets up and leaves.

Hanan

SHE'S THIRTY-FIVE YEARS OLD. In her free time, she enjoys drawing. She studies the wall and the city's buildings crammed together, then transposes all of this onto her canvas, sometimes with oils and other times with watercolors.

Her father passed away years earlier. She has one sister, Khadija, who is married to a fishmonger, and two older brothers, one of whom is an architect in the Emirates. The other is married to a Syrian woman and can't return to Jerusalem because the occupation forces have an arrest warrant out on him.

Her younger brother owns a store in Sydney and is married to an Australian. He visits Jerusalem once every three years and brings his mother and sisters silk handkerchiefs and gold bracelets.

Hanan's unhappiness with the world is not satisfied by silk or gold.

Her First Visit

HE ASKS HER, "Do you remember your first visit to this house? It was a week after our engagement. I brought you here in your thin pink dress and you climbed these steps like a deer, your dark hair draped over your shoulders. You greeted my mother and father, and my mother asked you, 'How can you wear that dress in the middle of winter?' You laughed and told her you weren't cold, and I joked that you'd caught the 'youth fever.' We sat in the living room. You hardly said a word, maybe because you were self-conscious of the dress, or maybe because it was the first time you'd been to our house. Then you joined my mother in the kitchen to make dessert. Remember?"

Khadija says, "I remember every detail. You were twenty-three."

~

A Meeting

RABAB COMES TO MY REGULAR COFFEE SHOP,
bringing with her some sheets of paper on which she has
written some of her poems. She wants me to read them
and leave comments.

Rabab has fascinated me since the evening I visited
with her father. I'm twenty years older than her but she
tells me that there's a mystery about me that the younger
guys who go to her school don't have. She tells me,
"There's a huge difference between a writer who has
read a thousand books and written hundreds of pages
and a university student who can't write a single good
paragraph."

I read one of her poems. I read and smile and express
my admiration for what she's written. She sits, drinking
coffee, and her heart, as it looks to me, is pounding. I can
hear my heart pounding as well.

∾

Birth

SHE SAYS that she gave birth to Rabab at a hospital. Abd el-Razzaq carried her into the car a little past noon. It was spring and Khadija's belly protruded so much it looked like she was having twins.

Rabab came out with little trouble and Khadija breastfed her, then put her to sleep, before Abd el-Razzaq came in to admire his daughter's face and say, "God bless her beauty."

An hour later, Rabab woke up, took her mother's breast, and both mother and daughter went back to sleep. Two days later, Khadija returned home, a beautiful baby girl in her arms. The house welcomed her every step as she climbed the stairs.

The Bird Keeper

A NEW DEVELOPMENT AWAITS ME. I'm pleased by the sensation and am in no hurry to go home, so I roam every market and walk every alley.

At this late hour the stores are all closed, and the few people remaining glide along, ghostlike. The city is lonely, and in each of its corners stand soldiers.

I stop by the house of my friend, the singer, who is entertaining many guests, all with a passion for music. My friend sings and plays the lute: "You flatter, you flatter, you charmer and sweet talker." His voice darkens. "The beauty of this country is in the glance of a girl and in the bloom of a rose. Bird Keeper, wake up and watch over your bird."

An hour later, as I leave the singer's house, the gentle sensation returns. In my horizon there awaits a familiar bird.

Marble

I LOWER MY HEAD onto her marble breasts. (Marble is a symbol of rebirth, the plaque beneath the sculpture declares.) She clings to me as if she's been waiting for this for a thousand years. She tells me, "There are many strangers here, and I feel cold."

I ask, "Shall I bring you wool blankets?"

"That is not what I desire."

"What is it that you desire?"

Glancing around hesitantly, she whispers, "For you not to forget that I'm here while you're out there."

Shahnaz

WALKING DOWN KATAMON STREET that day, I see Jewish women and their children walking on the sidewalk. I remember Virginia, the slender daughter of Bethlehem who moved with her parents to Jerusalem, to Katamon Street, into the house of Wasif Jawhariyyeh, who had a passion for composition and singing. Wasif played the lute and sang, while Virginia accompanied him skillfully.

Wasif later suggested a stage name that would better fit her future as a famous singer, and Virginia accepted it. Her name became Shahnaz.

Shahnaz sang in Jerusalem a few times before her body began to waste from some mysterious illness and she quit singing. The Jerusalem lute player remained depressed until the day he died because Shahnaz was his shining hope, a hope that was blown out as if it had never been. The Jewish women look around them as if they've heard Shahnaz's singing somewhere.

~

Sultana

WALKING DOWN KATAMON STREET, I remember Sultana, who moved into a new house on this street, where she lived for a few months until her illness took her. She'd wake up in the middle of the night, gasping for air. Her husband would open the window to let in a breeze, hold her with her head on his chest. He would feel her forehead, smooth her hair, and tell her stories to put her back to sleep.

After falling asleep, she'd wake up and remain awake until daybreak. He'd suggest he call the doctor but she wouldn't want to trouble him, so she'd tell him to wait until morning, when he'd put on his suit and fez and go looking for a doctor.

An hour later he'd return with the doctor, who would examine her while her husband stood staring at the body that only a month ago was beautiful. The doctor would pull a box of pills from his briefcase and hand it to him.

She'd sleep for two or three hours as he lay next to her, her broken body pressed against his, wishing death would take him first so he wouldn't have to see her die.

∽

A Picture

AS I WALK toward the house on Katamon Street, I remember her in the picture, standing in a long night-gown beside the wall's gate, waving good-bye to him on his way to work. He'd turn to her like a man who can't endure his darling wife being out of sight for a few hours.

She had a habit of waiting beside the gate to welcome him home from work in her light blue dress. He'd run up to her, embrace her, hold her, and they would walk inside together. Separated from her for a few hours, he felt as if he'd been away for a thousand years. Yes, he was crazy for Sultana.

Sultana is gone now and the only thing that remains of her are a few lines in a book, a wave good-bye, and the picture of a beautiful woman standing at the front door of the house, a house that is now lost.

Humidity

JANETTE WAS WALKING through the city when she saw him.

He knew all the passageways branching off the New Gate by heart and enjoyed the humidity of the alleyways, the stones of the houses. When she saw him, he was standing under one of those houses' windows, shoulder against the stones, holding the weapon given to him to defend the city. (He was a volunteer in a unit known as "the Red Belts.") The city lived under dull showers of bombs and bullets.

He stood under the window waiting for the woman he'd laid eyes on days earlier. He fell in love with her beauty and her purple dress, while she admired his height and posture.

They walked together as if they were engaged. When they found themselves in an empty alley, he pulled her to his chest and kissed her. She told him she was afraid. He told her not to be and led her out by the hand, and they continued walking.

Four weeks later, she remained in the city while he was buried under it.

⌒

Love

SHE WALKS through the city and remembers him.

He loved her and she loved him. He told her, "If I go to your house and ask your parents for your hand, would they approve?" She said, "Why wouldn't they? My father makes no distinction between one religion and another. What about your parents? Would they approve?" He answered, "Why wouldn't they?" She said, "Well, you are of one religion and I am of another." He said, "I don't care what my parents think. I do what I want."

A gentle breeze teased the purple dress adorning her tall, slender figure. She walked proudly next to her man who was defending his city, elated by every minute they spent together and oblivious of what was to come.

Mustafa walked beside her, unsure of the future. But they walked together as if their city was at peace.

Mustafa

ABD EL-RAZZAQ SAYS, "My uncle Mustafa died a martyr when I was two. My grandma said she tore her dress mourning him. That was 1948. She said he loved a girl named Janette, whom he brought over to the house three times. Her face was as beautiful as the moon and her body as supple as an olive branch. At times my grandma would pray, 'May God bless her. She is made of gold, inside and out.'

"Janette loved my uncle. They'd decided to get married. Grandma always remembered her and would say tearfully, 'My heart breaks for your loss, Mustafa.'

"My grandma visited my uncle's grave on holidays for years and looked at his name inscribed on the tombstone. She shed tears remembering him and Janette, and how they were so compatible."

~

Janette

SHE WALKS to the all-girls school.

She leaves her house in the Christian Quarter and heads to the Damascus Gate, seeing the school building standing ahead, where she has worked as an Arabic literature teacher and worn black for a year. She went into mourning when her lover was killed—a bullet found him as he patrolled the wall, protecting the city from its enemies.

She remembers his good looks and the evening he held her to him. She says she will never forget him, and now she wears black.

All day, she's busy giving the girls language lessons, and in the evening her lover's specter comes, bringing her only sorrow.

~

The Mortuary

YORAM READS from the old document:

*The Christians of Jerusalem worked as blacksmiths, craft-
ing both farming tools, such as sickles and axes, and building tools, such as hammers and levels. They also made
cookware, such as metal buckets and trays; cutlery, such as
forks and knives; and houseware, such as metal chairs and
metal bed frames.*

> *. . .*

> *Our records describe a blacksmith shop in the Damas-
cus Gate neighborhood, run by the master blacksmith Elias,
son of . . . Issa al-Rizk, . . . and Badr el-Din al-Aklil. The
master blacksmith Abd el-Nour, son of Botrous, purchased
from the master blacksmith Elias, son of Issa al-Rizk, . . .
a percentage of the business for four hundred piasters, and
then Badr el-Din al-Aklil returned after one year and
purchased Abd el-Nour's share in the business for the same
amount of money.*

Yoram begins to cough. He worries about the blacksmith shop that the Palestinians might use to build pipes
for their rockets, so he sends some of his men over to
search the shop and arrest Elias, Badr el-Din, and Abd

el-Nour, all of them, anticipating they will certainly find suspicious metal objects in the shop.

Yoram applauds his relentless and sharp eye.

Hookah

HE SAYS, "We can no longer sit on our own porch. The porch was my and my wife's favorite place. We would sit close together, she in the nightgown she wears after dinner and I in my pajamas and the abaya my friend gave me. The hookah in front of me would bubble in the stillness of the night as my wife would lay her head on my shoulder and tell me that the hookah's bubbling was making her sleepy.

"But we can't sit on the porch anymore now that those five have come along. Sometimes twenty of them show up. They occupy a nearby house and go out on the porch, and seeing them standing there is enough to ruin our mood. My wife goes back inside and I follow her moments later, leaving the hookah silent and cold on the porch."

Like a Widow

HANAN LEAVES the architecture office in the evening. She walks the streets upset—strangers are taking control of the city.

Jerusalem mourns, empty in the evening, her markets stuffed, in places, with trash and plastic bags.

Hanan walks into her house exhausted, a mother of seven who rushes home to feed her children and put them each to bed with goodnight kisses, then take her sweaty and troubled body into the bathroom. Hanan undresses, showers, and walks out of the bathroom in a cotton robe.

She lies in bed. She stretches, and her robe unravels from her body. In a moment of vulnerability, a bitter feeling takes over, one of abandonment. She feels like an orphan—like a widow without friends.

~

Glass

THEY SHARE A BED, and their whispers fill the room. They expose, in a moment of contentment, their little secrets to the fragile world, to an unsafe city, to a house nearing oblivion. And they hold each other as if they fear some danger will separate them.

They lie in bed stripped of worry and resentment, living unhurried in this temporary bliss. And they confide in one another: she, how she loves to be near him in the quiet of the night, and he, how he loves her young body.

There they are, in complete harmony, when a rock hits their bedroom windowpane. Unrest and anger follow.

~

A Feeling

SHE SAYS the broken window appears sad and the house looks as if it were in pain, incapable of moving past what happened. She walks out into the street and grabs a handful of rocks, then climbs up to the roof and throws the rocks at the occupied house. Nothing breaks, as the windows of the occupied house are covered with barbed wire.

Abd el-Razzaq returns after half an hour with a carpenter to replace the glass. An hour later, Khadija is alone in the house, unable to shake the feeling that the house is unwell. She brings the garden hose inside, lifts her skirt over her legs and tucks it into her underwear, and washes the windows and the old colored marble, and the floor tiles, and the kitchen, and the bathroom.

She does not rest until she feels the house regain its balance.

~

At Play

ASMAHAN WOULD PLAY her favorite game whenever her mother scrubbed the floors. The waves of water mixing with soap sliding across the marble tempted her, so she would sit down and push her small body forward, sending it gliding across the hallway. She didn't care that her clothes got wet, and her mother let her get soaked.

When she finished scrubbing the floors, her mother would lead her by the hand to the bathroom, strip and bathe her, and dress her in clean clothes before herself undressing to spend a long time in the shower.

Asmahan, now that she's reached puberty, can no longer play her favorite game. She must help her mother scrub the floors and settle for getting her feet wet as she mops, pushing the water toward the bathroom. After cleaning and drying the marble floors, she unwinds with a comfortable bath.

The Wedding Night

HE ASKS HER, "Do you remember our wedding night? I came and got you from your father's house with a *zaffa* band playing and the neighborhood women ululating and singing. You took your first step inside this house while the weather was cold. You weren't my first wife and I wasn't your first husband, either. Do you remember the kiss that was shaded with reluctance? What was going through your mind then? What was going through mine?

"We went to Jericho the next day for our honeymoon. Jericho's heat was a welcome change from the unbearable cold our bodies had endured. A month later, we came home and spring was on our doorstep. Do you remember?"

Khadija says, "I remember every detail. We were so shy at first. Then we became like two goats loose in a field."

∽

Suspicions

SUSPICION GNAWS AT YORAM. He sits reading an article about the Lebanese journalist Salim Sarkis, residing in Egypt, who had visited Jerusalem in 1923. He infiltrated its hotels and written about their bad service: "Take, for instance, the Grand New Hotel, also known as the Locanda Dance Hall. It would have been recognized as a hotel twenty-five years ago, but now everything about it screams, 'The world has advanced, but these drapes and chairs and tables and dining tables and bells and service and napkins, etc.—they are all antique.'"

Yoram has to put down his newspaper for a second, trembling with anger, then picks it up again. "The Locanda Dance Hall is fascinating in its operation. One would usually walk up to the front desk and ask for a newspaper. But no, before the word newspaper can come out of one's mouth, a newspaper is shoved under one's nose. Typically newspapers are sent up to a person's room or placed on the dining table."

Yoram sends the newspaper flying across the room, where it settles on a pile of papers. He's convinced his suspicions are grounded—this journalist was a spy sent here to ruin the tourist season the country was eagerly anticipating.

Yoram decides to place Salim Sarkis's name on airport and border checklists so that the appropriate procedures will be taken against him the moment he arrives in the country. Yoram is not aware that Sarkis has been dead for years. He prefers to adopt his own way of doing things, his own philosophy, which he refuses to disclose to a soul, no matter how highly he regards the person.

~

Disclosure

I SAY TO HER, "My first wife stayed ten years with me and gave me a child, but we were different people. I am okay with a little mess and laziness, but she couldn't stand it." I tell her, "I love a woman who knows when to cuddle in a man's lap like a pigeon, and when to give him space. I have a temper, you see, and I get angry when something ticks me off." Rabab says she's willing to live with my moodiness. I hold her hand in the Damascus Gate Café, the one with the patio umbrellas.

Her body feels deliciously tingly, she later tells me, when I ask her to marry me. She says she's in love with my directness. And the owner sits in his coffee shop right now, waiting for the unimaginable, trying to devise a solution to the coming troubles.

Prayer

"I WASHED FOR PRAYER, and so did Khadija. Then we prayed to God that he would bring him back to us," he says. "Emigration took him from us and we've received only one letter from him. He didn't include a return address, so we couldn't write back to check on him. I stood up, putting myself in the hands of the Lord, and Khadija stood behind me, ready for prayer. We implored him: 'We will soon be expelled from our house. What should we do? Speak to us, our dear son, who has left us and walked into the unknown!' We pleaded with him: 'Come back to us. If they force us to evacuate our house, we will face disaster.'

"We told him all this, standing in the hands of the Lord while his mother mixed pleading words with warm tears that slipped from her eyes during and after prayer."

~

A Body

RABAB AND I STROLL. (We're staying in the city for our honeymoon.) The city embraces us like children to her bosom, and we walk slowly in the valley of her breasts. We approach the house occupied by Sharon. We see the flags of white and blue on the roof. I tell her, "They occupied the heart of the city, do you see?"

She nods and says, "The city's chest is exposed to the wind and rain and to strangers, now." I say that the valley road we're walking on used to be a deep trench where fighters met, but it was later filled with rocks and dirt. She nods and says, "Here, to the right, was a cafeteria, and to the left, a restaurant." I say, "Here, on the left, was a church, and further on, a mosque." She says, "And there, far to the right, was a mosque and a church and domes." And I say, "Here was water and marble, and there was water and marble."

The city lies on its back with one leg to the right and another to the left. The valley is filled with fornicators, and Rabab and I walk down the road until we nearly reach its end.

A Puzzle

WE'RE IN BED, she on the right and I on the left. She reads a book about al-Niffari and tells me that the Sufi language takes her to mysterious places. I read a Hodja comic. I chuckle and say, "Listen to this:

"Hodja walked up to some people with a plum in his sleeve and told them, 'Whoever guesses what is up my sleeve wins the biggest plum.' They all said, 'A plum.' He said, 'Whoever gave that away is a son of a bitch!'"

We laugh, then she sets her book down, sliding closer to me, and says, "Tonight I'm troubled by the uncertainty in our future." I set my book down and tell her, "Come closer. I will ease your troubled mind, or make it worse."

~

Abd el-Rahman

SHE SAYS she gave birth to Abd el-Rahman in the winter. His mood is as unpredictable as the season he was born in. He had a temper ever since he was a kid and nothing would calm him down more than taking his anger out on the furniture. He would break the dishes and glasses, flip the chairs and sofas, and throw the pillows out the window. He would not stop assaulting the furniture until his anger had run out.

She says, "Abd el-Rahman grew up with a bad temper. The house put up with him because the house is patient and has a big heart."

Their Eldest Son

HE SAYS, "Nothing. Not a letter, not a word. If only he would send us one letter! If only he would send a word! I can't fathom how cities can swallow men whole like that. Could it be that a city in France or Germany or Belgium has swallowed him and left no time for him to remember his mother and father, or his two sisters and brother?

"I don't understand. How can a woman have control over a man like that, that he would think only of her and no one else? He's devoted to her night and day.

"Maybe that's not it. Maybe the city has not swallowed him and the woman does not control him. Maybe he made friends with the wrong people and got himself killed. Maybe he got arrested for some felony and was sent to prison. If he were in prison, though, he would've written to us.

"Not a letter or a word. No phone call or notice. His mother and I live in the hope of hearing from him."

Her First Pregnancy

HE ASKS HER, "Do you remember the first time you were pregnant, and how happy we were that you carried a baby that would soon be born, any day now? I wanted it to be a boy so badly. My first wife was with me for ten years and didn't give me a boy.

"Do you remember how I used to talk to your belly? I used to sit and stare at your belly and think how beautiful it was, like a white dome. We used to move our bed from one corner to the next in the bedroom because you wanted a change of scenery. Do you remember that?"

Khadija says, "I remember every detail. You were in awe at how full my belly was. You would bow down to it like a worshipper in a temple."

A Smell

HE'S SUMMONED to the intelligence officer's office. The officer gives him a cold calm stare and Ghazal shakes in his boots. His face turns red, then yellow, and he can't stop shaking.

The officer says, "We know everything there is to know about you."

He stands there, trembling, as he turns from red to yellow. The officer says to him, "You will cooperate." Ghazal feels uncomfortable and confused. The officer, pointing to a paper, says, "Sign your name here."

Suddenly Ghazal has trouble digesting his lunch. "May I go to the bathroom?" he asks, completely humiliated. "Sign here, then you may go to the bathroom," the officer answers.

Ghazal signs his name, then grabs his stomach and dashes to the bathroom. A strong odor emanates from inside the bathroom, and Ghazal feels better.

At night, his wife, lying next to him, says, "Something smells bad."

He tells her to shut up, then turns his back to her and falls asleep.

Yoram

YORAM RETURNS HOME one night and looks around, searching for foreign knights. He has grown used to seeing them in the city, but every time he's close to arresting or shooting one of them, they disappear. Yoram is saddened by the strange state the city is in.

He approaches his house's garden and sees a man coming out the front door. He is definitely his double. Yoram draws his gun and fires one shot (no need to waste more than one bullet), but his double walks away uninjured. His wife steps out, and the neighbors stick their heads out their windows.

The double disappears and Yoram returns his gun to its holster. He prepares himself for the long conversation he knows his wife will want to have.

A Crisis

GHAZAL MEETS A GIRL from Florida named Meryl. He proposes to take her on a tour of the old city. She agrees and they walk side by side. He's elated every time an acquaintance sees him walking next to her.

But then, unexpectedly, he feels indigestion. He tries to control it until he reaches the public bathroom at the end of the market. He urges Meryl to walk faster and she does. When he excuses himself to use the bathroom, he finds the door locked.

Ghazal is in big trouble. He sprints to a side alley, and relieves himself while shielding his face from some kids who are playing nearby. Meryl waits for him, but then the stench reaches her, and she leaves.

~

Meryl

GHAZAL MISSES MERYL. He's surprised to find her one day sitting in a café by the hospital. He asks her to lunch at a nearby restaurant and she accepts. She asks him up to her hotel room and he accepts. He enters into her room, proud as a rooster. She asks him to kiss her feet. He's hesitant at first, and then consents to do it, but he thinks to himself, "If only she was considerate enough to run cold water over them."

He kisses her feet for a week, then Meryl disappears again.

He keeps looking for her, eager to kiss her ivory and silver feet.

The Jilbāb

SHE MAKES COFFEE, pouring me a cup and one for herself. I drink my coffee quietly as she stares at me lying in bed, until she says, "Do you have a date with a new poem today?" I reply sharply that I don't.

She doesn't like my abrupt answer. I ask her, "Did you remove your *jilbāb* on one of your trips?"

"Which *jilbāb*?"

"The one you used to wear at your parents' house."

"I had a *jilbāb* but I didn't wear it at my parents' house."

I stared at her a moment longer, then said, "Rabab, why are you lying to me?"

"I'm not lying to you."

We return to sipping our coffee. Hands bring the small cups up and bring them back down, while in her mind and mine, exclamation marks are being drawn and redrawn.

And the *jilbāb* that Rabab says she didn't wear is hanging somewhere.

∽

The Man

I'M TAKING A WALK with Rabab when we see him. As we follow him, Rabab wonders if he's the doppelgänger, but I say he's Saladin, and that we've been transported to the Ayyubid era.

We see him going through the Damascus Gate and then descending the stairs in the market with three men trailing him. His sword hangs from his waist to his ankle.

It's summer and the market is steeped in lantern light. The man strides with a firm step around the men standing outside one of the stores swapping stories, one telling of the daughter of a foreigner who ran away with a local merchant. Everyone stands there wordlessly for a moment after he finishes telling his story before comments and debates erupt. The women sit outside a house listening to the men's conversations, and lean against each other to whisper intimately.

Silence dominates the city soon after, and the stars glimmer. The moon is absent from the sky.

Saladin enters al-Aqsa Square and dismisses the guards with a wave of his hand. He sits alone and contemplates all that the city has undergone, as well as what is yet to come, while the city talks for weeks about the girl who ran away with one of the local merchants.

An Arrest

I KNOW NOTHING of his secret affairs. We sit chatting and drinking coffee one evening in Café Groppi on Sultan Suleiman the Magnificent Street. He says he was summoned for questioning one day and stood there shaking, hands damp as a wet cloth.

I pity his weakness and wonder how it's served him in his life. After a long conversation, he asks me about the soon-to-be-evacuated house in the Old City. He asks what we can do to get out of the situation we're in. I suggest he join the protest we'll have in a few days, and his face goes pale.

The day after the protest, officers and soldiers surround my house and take me to a hellhole where they place me under arrest for three months.

A detective with a shiny bald head bombards me with one question after another. Ghazal is there. He isn't there in person, but he's there.

Thirst

SHE WAKES UP with a fright and rushes to turn the light on. He rouses, rubbing his eyes, and looks at her. "What's wrong with you, woman?"

She says, "I saw him tiptoe through the front door, careful not to wake us up. I saw him. He went into the kitchen, opened the fridge, and took out a water bottle. My dear boy! He was so thirsty! He's seen some hard times in that foreign land. He must be very hungry. I'm going to make him some food."

"Sleep, woman. Don't be silly. Only God knows where he is now."

"I'll make him some food and then go back sleep. He might still come during the night or early in the morning."

She puts on her lilac robe and goes into the kitchen. Abd el-Razzaq pulls the sheets over his head and tries to sleep.

Rejection

HE SAYS, "I kept trying to help, but then I got tired of it. I suggested he marry the butcher's daughter, but he refused. He said the same thing he always does, that evil is everywhere and that he will not get married in such a world as this."

She says, "I visited the butcher and met his daughter and examined her up close. How pretty she is, God bless her. She has a strong firm body and thighs like marble. Her teeth are little pearls and her hair comes down to her waist. God bless her, she's perfect!"

She describes her to Abd el-Rahman, hoping to persuade him to marry her. He says evil is everywhere, so he will not get married, and that, more than anything, he misses his brother.

God help him, Abd el-Rahman refuses to listen. And when he's finished praying, he asks forgiveness for his mother and father, for they don't know how to please him.

~

Stairs

THE MARKET is sloped like a ladder leaning against a wall. They walk up the stairs together, up one hundred steps before he stops. She says, "How many stairs left?" He answers, "Four hundred." She asks, "Are you in a hurry?" He says no. So Suzanne pulls her friend down to sit and says, "Let's rest a little before we walk up the remaining four hundred steps."

≈

The Spice Traders Market

SHE WALKS through the Spice Traders Market and I walk alongside her. She's been out of prison for only two days, so I take her to buy whatever she wants.

The market is quiet and smells of spices and peppers and herbs. She buys black cumin, cinnamon, ground pepper, ginger, and *oud*, and other things she has read about in an old book about our ancestors. She looks at me tenderly now. I stand beside her, an obedient child.

We go home and the delicious scents cling to us for days and weeks. Rabab transforms into Scheherazade at night and burns incense in our bedroom, saying the sweetest words to me.

A Chair

I GO to the antique furniture store and find a wooden chair that's a hundred years old. (Maybe it was made by a skilled carpenter for an Ottoman sultan.) I also find an old map, a spoon made of copper and another of silver, and coffee cups with beautiful designs. I consider a piece of embroidered colored cloth.

I return home excited to show Rabab what I've bought and ask her opinion, at which she purses her lips. We talk for some time and decide that we're happy with some of the objects (like the map). I busy myself looking for spots to put the antiques, resolved to find the perfect place to display each of them to draw our guests' utmost admiration.

In the evening, I sit down on the hundred-year-old wooden chair and Rabab sits next to me. I fancy myself an uncrowned sultan, Rabab my modern-day sultana.

Coffee

I WONDER as I'm making the coffee, "What should I do with my heart tonight?" But I can't come up with an answer, nor is my mood cooperating. Rabab has gone out.

As the coffee boils over and drips into the fire, I wonder again what I should do. I don't feel like speaking or watching the news or laughing, nor am I in the mood to go out and watch the setting sun as it spreads gold across the sky. I am not in the mood for anything at all.

Despair surrounds me, stirs in me ashen feelings of doubt and sadness.

Eventually I raise the coffee cup to my lips. For the tenth time, I wonder what I should do tonight.

Wardrobe

I OPEN THE WARDROBE: dresses, blouses, underwear, pantyhose, corsets. The clothes release a fragrance, as if trying to seduce me, and I hurriedly look around. Finding no one, I continue looking for the jilbāb.

I push the dresses aside and start sifting through the pile of underwear, pantyhose, and corsets, but I soon stop because there's no way the jilbāb will be hidden among the underwear and pantyhose. It will have to be with the dresses. I check each dress once, twice, and even a third time, but I still can't find the jilbāb.

I close the door and sit down by the window, trying to recall the details of this old memory, but I can't remember.

~

Belongings

I RETURN HOME carrying antiques: an old bag made from colorfully embroidered cloth, an antique silver ink bottle and quill, an embossed metal cup, and an oval mirror with a copper base. I display them on the dining table as a street salesman and Rabab watches me, smiling.

"What, why are you smiling?"

"Soon we're going to look like we live in Eugène Ionesco's *The New Tenant*."

"Oh! So you're worried we won't have room to set a foot in this house if I keep buying antiques?"

"How much did you buy this for?"

"Guess."

"I don't know a thing about how much this stuff costs."

A certain anecdote comes to mind and I tell her, "They say that, years ago, Hodja ran into some boys playing with a dead crow. So he bought it from them and carried it home. His mother asked why he bought a dead crow and he said, 'Because if it was alive, it wouldn't have been worth a hundred dirham.'"

Rabab laughs and we go on displaying the antiques—in the living room, in the bathroom, in the kitchen, and by the bed. She looks at herself in the mirror by the bed and says, "I wish you would buy us another mirror like this one." She doesn't say another word for the rest of the night.

Foothold

WE'RE IN BED. Rabab is reading Eugène Ionesco's *The New Tenant* and I'm reading Attar of Nishapur's "The Conference of the Birds." Suddenly I stop and turn to her. "Did you say 'a foothold' today?"

"I did. Why?"

"Are you really afraid that we won't have a foothold in this house one day?"

"Yeah. With all the antiques you bring home, soon there won't even be room to set a foot down."

She gets out of bed while telling me that the weather is too warm. She stands by the window, and I think to myself how beautiful she looks, silhouetted in her nightgown. She stares vacantly at the lights coming in through the window from the settlements spreading north and south, east and west, and whispers, "I'm afraid."

I get up and move beside her to place a hand on her shoulder, and we stand by the window until we are too weary to stay upright.

Souk al-Dabbagha

WE GO TOGETHER to Souk al-Dabbagha. She tells me she wants to buy a handbag made of genuine leather, so we enter a store not far from the Church of the Holy Sepulchre, near a small mosque only thirty feet or so long. She examines the handbags presented by the salesman, then reaches toward this and that shelf and takes down other handbags of all shapes. The salesman tells her, "I have handbags from the Ayyubid time." She looks at him in astonishment. "Really?"

I'm not surprised. No, I expect this reaction from her. The salesman tells her to go upstairs to the second floor to see for herself, so Rabab does. The salesman walks up after her, and I follow them upstairs.

She spends half an hour upstairs going through the Ayyubid handbags before finally deciding on a fringed one. She lifts it over her shoulder and we walk out.

Outside, we see a knight of Saladin wearing a copper helmet, a Yamani sword slung at his side. A woman paces beside him, delicate as a white dove. She gazes through the glass window of the handbag store of an Armenian salesman from Jerusalem who'd lived during the mandate.

On-Screen

SHE SAYS she saw him on TV. He had a kaffiyeh around his neck and carried a four-colored flag over his head. He was surrounded by women and men calling for the end of the occupation. She says, "I was so happy to see him, I wept. I miss my son."

He asks her if she's sure it was their son.

"I'm positive. It was Marwan."

"They say that everyone has a twin."

"No, no, no! It was Marwan."

"Do you know what country the demonstration was in?"

"Europe."

He smiles at her. "Khadija, Europe is a continent. It's much bigger than you think."

He adds nothing but remains skeptical of what his wife told him, so skeptical that he sits fixed in front of the television all week, looking for his son night and day.

Unfortunately, the demonstrations suddenly stop. He slaps his knee and thinks, "God Almighty, you'd think all the problems have finally been solved!"

~

A Spoon

EVERY EVENING, I write my daily report for the newspaper and then, in the morning, I read the paper in its entirety, starting with the obituaries and finishing with the events page. I don't dwell on politics, in the paper or anywhere else.

Each week, I make lunch three days and she the other three. When we sit down to eat together, one of us always takes a sheet or two of the newspaper and drapes it over the dining table like a tablecloth. We eat and look at the photographs of the actresses and singers and soccer players, and the pictures don't move even when bones and crumbs of rice fall on them. It's at these moments we're most compatible.

We fight over the silliest things, like when Rabab folds up the newspapers after lunch, just as they are. The crumbs and the bones and even my favorite spoon are still on them, and she just tosses all of it into the trash. (I only realize the spoon is missing the next day or the day after.) Because of this I'm forced to form a new bond with a new spoon of quality I neither like nor want.

Her Little Girl

SHE SAYS she gave birth to Asmahan in the fall (in October, to be exact), in the evening when the weather was moderate.

Like the weather in which she was born, Asmahan is calm by nature. She's tall and slim. She likes to listen more than speak but within her is bottled-up energy waiting to be released. She reminds me of her younger days, when she was a little girl first coming to grips with life around her.

She says, "I raised Rabab in this house. I thought she was the last grape from the vine and I gave her so much love and affection. But Asmahan's birth, too, brought unexpected and great joy to our home."

Her Grandson's Coat

SHE'S BUSY KNITTING a small wool sweater for a one-year-old boy. He asks as he approaches her, "What, are we expecting another baby?" She smiles and says, "Sure."

"Is Rabab pregnant?"

"Rabab isn't thinking about kids right now."

"Then who?"

"It's Marwan."

He remembers his son, roaming somewhere in the world. He could be alive, or he could be dead, and, if alive, he doesn't even know if his son is married. Does he have children? His eyes darken with melancholy.

Looking up at Khadija and the little sweater, he advises her not to tire herself making a coat for a baby that might not exist.

Khadija disagrees and goes on knitting the tiny sweater for her grandson. She's heard from many people that winter in Europe demands warm clothing. She'll send her grandson the sweater somehow, unless her grandson comes home soon with his mother and father.

Walking

WE WALK TOGETHER from one market to the next, Rabab in an elegant dress with her hair down, I in a white button-up shirt and gray pants. Rabab watches people shop in the markets as if it's her first time there. Occasionally her eyes glide over the myriad doors and windows of the houses. I try not to break her concentration, walking beside her as if it's our first time together, reminiscing now and then of the city's ancient shops.

Two hours later she says, "Let's go home." We do, and on the way I imagine her composing in her mind a poem about the city. So I walk beside her in silence, trying to control my loud thoughts and keep them from intruding on the poem forming in her mind.

∽

Sunday

SHE ROAMS the old alleys with a book about the history of the city in her hand, inspecting the walls and the doors of the houses with careful eyes. She likes the Ayyubid architecture evident in the long walls of a dim alley leading up to an illuminated open space, which then connects with the courtyard of a house. She stops more than once and attentively rereads the pages of her book.

Around that time, her friend, who interns at the law office, meets up with her. They greet one another and continue wandering together. They walk up and down many flights of stairs in alleyways and markets as the church bells ring, synchronized and harmonious.

Barefoot

SHE TELLS ME when she gets tired of my jokes, "Why don't you take off your slippers and come sit on my lap?"

"I'm barefoot."

"Why don't you sit on my lap, then?"

"I'm going to go look for my slippers."

"Don't go too far."

I walk too far and when I return, I find her sleeping. I sit by her feet, still barefoot.

≈

The City Bells

THE CITY BELLS RING in the morning as the churches welcome worshippers. Entering the church, men and women all grow lighter—the men shedding their heavy winter coats and the women the burdens of their worries and losses.

The bells ring loud, as if in protest. They demand we think of the trying times the city has come upon. After making their demands, the ringing gradually subsides.

This morning, one bell broke the mold and kept on ringing until sundown.

Khan Tankaz

SHE SAYS she misses sleeping in the Old City and suggests we visit her parents, and is surprised when I suggest instead that we go to the time of Khan Tankaz and spend a night there.

She packs the white nightgown embroidered with red roses, a pair of underwear, and her perfume and makeup, and I pack my grey pajamas. We pack some books and carry a suitcase, as if we're headed to the airport.

We cross the Damascus Gate just as the king's guards are about to close it. We continue walking in the night and turn down the road leading to al-Aqsa Mosque. Lanterns light the streets and storefronts where some merchants still sit. Rabab is utterly taken by the city that has yet to fall asleep.

At Alqtanin Market, the entrance is wide and beautiful, with delicate carvings, arches, and colorful stones. We take a left and enter the roofed market. After travelling a short distance in the market, we take another left turn and reach Khan Tankaz. We see men and women from distant lands who have come to sleep in Khan Tankaz and find the man in charge to ask him for a room. He hands us a key, shows us to our room, and wishes us a good night's rest.

We stay awake until midnight, though we truly do have a good night's rest. In the morning, we must walk seven hundred years to get back to our house outside the city wall.

~

Bread

HANAN INVITES HIM to her house to meet her mother. He eats the bread of the house, comfortably looking left and right, as if he were seated at the dinner table in his own home. Every now and then, a laugh slips from between his lips. His white teeth show.

He has the laugh of an innocent child, he, who has traveled the long road away from innocence.

His stomach feels heavy and that spoils his mood, so he stands up and prepares to leave so he can unburden himself of the weight in his stomach. He tries to let out a fake guileless laugh but fails for the first time, maybe because his behavior has exposed something unbearable in his character.

Pain

SHE WRITES A POEM about the city. She reads it for the sixth time and feels as if she is alive again, uniting the city's pain with hers.

She tears up the poem and rewrites it for the seventh time, because the city's pain is much graver than her own, more massive than her senses can grasp.

～

News Broadcast

HIS EYES FOLLOW HER, in her light blue dress. She moves gracefully between the living room and kitchen, returning with cookies and tea and glasses to sit beside him on the sofa, and he feels at home.

He asks her, "Why don't we take a walk?"

"In the state this city's in?"

"Yeah, in this state. If we stay trapped in this house, we'll explode."

"I'm already trapped in this house. You get to go to the store every morning and spend your day there."

"Why don't you visit me at the store, then? You can sit with me and watch my customers. You might have fun."

She smiles at him. "Ha. And the housework? Who's going to take care of that?"

She pours tea into the cups, content to have made her point, but he revisits the conversation.

Interrupting him, she calls for Asmahan. Abd el-Rahman is out of the house and will not be home until a little after midnight. Asmahan comes out of her room and sits beside her mother and father. Each affectionately caresses her hair, and before they can say anything, the news comes on.

A Desire

SHE'S BEEN WAITING a long time and Ghazal still hasn't proposed. She told him she was okay with his keeping his first wife, and he promised to marry her in the fall. (That was last summer.) She tells him she yearned for a child who will have his height and eyes. His ego inflates, sitting there, listening. She goes to the market one day and buys a maternity dress for women in late-term pregnancy, and when she returns home she wraps cloth around her belly as if motherhood has already called on her. She puts the dress on slowly so as not to disturb the baby forming in her belly. She stands in front of the mirror and becomes aroused, staring at her body.

She rushes to the phone to call Ghazal and ask him to come over right away, but he doesn't answer.

Persistence

IN HIS FREE TIME, Yoram reads everything to do with the history of the city. He is troubled by many things of the city's past and wishes it could all simply be wiped away. Couldn't the authors of history just obliviate the things that trouble him? Then the city could return to him, pure and fully worthy of his respect.

Yoram is troubled by the city's long history of wars and destruction. He's bothered by the fact that it was destroyed and rebuilt seven times, and wonders, *will the city be destroyed an eighth time? Impossible.* Yoram stops reading to don the armor of a medieval knight from the Fatimid Caliphate. He mounts his horse hurriedly and ventures out into the city to protect it from further chaos and destruction.

A Suspect

ABD EL-RAHMAN is currently under arrest. They didn't believe him when he said he'd retired from life and retreated from people. He was too quiet, suspiciously quiet, and they suspected he was hiding something. Fearing he might leave them, his secrets still his own, they arrested him. They didn't want to regret letting him go free with his secrets.

Under the cover of night, they raided the house and found him reading the Qur'an. They searched his home—separated his father, mother, and sister, placed them all in different corners of the house—and finally searched him separately. They went into Suzanne's room and searched it, but found nothing suspicious in her bedroom, or in the kitchen, or in the bathroom, or in the attic over the bathroom.

They handcuffed him and led him away to prison as his mother cried out after him to be safe. She will have to wait for visitation hours at the prison to see him.

Asmahan

ASMAHAN SHIVERS as she watches the soldiers ravage their house. Her father tries to calm her, pulling her to him by her waist. "Don't be afraid."

Asmahan is afraid, not for herself but for Abd el-Rahman. She fears they'll shoot him, and when she hears a gunshot she freezes, brings her hands up to her ears, and shrinks into a corner.

Asmahan can't control her fear as the soldiers move from one room to the next, carelessly throwing things around. Her mother tries to calm her, too, and tenderly squeezes her hands.

But the girl can't bear the scene playing out in front of her. Through the mist of her panic she doesn't notice the yellow trickle making its way down her leg, running out into the middle of the room.

The commander stands there for a moment, then he and his officers leave, taking Abd el-Rahman with them.

A Dream

THE PREVIOUS NIGHT, she dreamed that she saw Ghazal walking in the markets of the city with a crow on his head. She decides to look for him so he can explain this dream to her. Maybe she'll find him roaming the markets.

She puts on her best clothes and lets her hair fall over her chest, then sprays on her favorite perfume and, inhaling deeply, walks out of her house.

Her perfume hangs in the air of every market of the city. She passes through the Bazaar Souk, Souk al-Dabbagha, the Spice Traders Market, Souk Khan el-Zeit, al-Wad Street, and Aqabat al-Saraya Street. In one of the markets, she hears a merchant from Ottoman times call out to her, inviting her to his store to browse through his collection of wool and fleeces, but she refuses because she doesn't have time.

She continues to search for him, to search far for him, on Avtimos Boulevard, in the Christian Quarter, in the Alloun Market, and at the Jaffa Gate. But she can't find him in the bustling city. The crow on his head continues to trouble her.

She keeps searching for him, searching far for him, but she can't find him.

She returns home sad. Three men harassed her as she looked for him.

A Hug

SHE SITS BESIDE ME and says, "I am not the same Rabab you've written your story about."

"And what makes you think that?"

"Because we didn't know each other when you wrote it."

I pull her to my chest and say, "Well, let's start a blank page, then." With emotion, I add, "Even if it were you who wore the jilbāb and went to the distant woods, I don't care about any of that now."

She relaxes into my embrace, and my body relaxes with and into hers.

Now, this doesn't mean I won't bring up the jilbāb incident again. Because I will, and it will lead to a fight which will be followed by a compromise made to render our lives tolerable again.

∽

Separation

SUZANNE LEAVES JERUSALEM one morning. Her attempts to remain in the city finally proved unsuccessful. A young Israeli employee at one of the agencies told her that she should leave the city right away.

She carries her luggage and some mementos from the city and returns to Marseille. She sleeps at night now and dreams that she's walking through the same markets she still loves. She wakes up every morning and calls her friends to tell them of her new dream about the city that stands forever alone. She does so often, because it's the only thing that can render the bitterness of separation somewhat tolerable.

⌒

The Butchers' Market

SHE WALKS through the Butchers' Market one afternoon. Blood covers the market floors and the stench is intolerable.

He's surprised to see her standing by the market's gate. He thinks she's her doppelgänger, who shows up sometimes for really no reason at all. (His wife has never come to this market before.)

Suddenly he remembers he suggested that she visit him and welcomes her, "Come in! Hello!" He takes hold of her hand and leads her inside. Awkwardly he offers her a chair. She sits down and watches him sell fish to his customers. She feels comfortable.

He only has time to speak to her again twenty minutes later. He apologizes, and she accepts his apology.

A Sofa

I ARRIVE HOME with a mover who hauls on his back a couch I've recently bought from an antique furniture store. I know she won't like the couch and how much room it will take up in the house, so I tell the mover, "Go first and deliver this to the lady of the house. I'll follow you in later."

I hide in the garden until Rabab has absorbed most of the shock, then I go inside with my hands held up high in surrender.

"Where are you going to put this disaster?"

"I thought we could put it by our bed. We could sit on it together and I could listen to you read me poetry."

I push the couch closer to the bed and sit on it like a sultan. I tell her to come closer, reminding her that there's enough room on the couch for her to sit beside me. But she refuses to sit down and stays mad at me.

I remember an anecdote of Nasreddin Hodja and say, "So, they say that one time Hodja bought a big bag of flour and, when he loaded it on the mover's back, the mover ran away with it. Days later, when Hodja ran into the mover, Hodja quickly ducked away from him. When asked why he hid from the mover, Hodja said, 'I'm worried he might ask me for his moving fee.'"

She laughs and says, "I wish the mover you hired had run away with this couch. I'd rather he do that than have to see it swallow up the entire space."

That night as she reads her poem, she lounges on the couch and tells me that I'm right to buy antiques (some of them, at least).

Swallowing Up the Place

I ASK HER IN BED, "Earlier, did you say that the couch swallowed up the place?"

"I did."

I can tell she doesn't want to talk for some reason.

Half an hour later, she goes back to being chatty. "If it was only the couch we had to worry about swallowing up the house, then it wouldn't be a big deal."

"I know what you mean. They're swallowing up the whole city." She doesn't add anything else.

Again silent, I'm happy to lie there, caressing her hair spread out on the pillow.

She's happy with what she said, and darkness soon takes over.

Tourism

YORAM AGAIN READS from an old document, this one dating back to the late nineteenth century:

> *The large number of pilgrims flooding into the city has led to the opening of new hotels, built to absorb this massive influx of visitors to Jerusalem. Some of these hotels are the private Locanda of Nathaniel, son of mister Thomas Mrad, the Protestant clock smith, located by the Jaffa Gate; the public Locanda Dance Hall, near the Roman monastery; and the private Locanda Vile, which, like the Locanda of Nathaniel, is also located by the Jaffa Gate.*
>
> . . .
>
> *The pilgrims come to Jerusalem before the Easter holiday to take part in the celebrations and rituals held in the city. They visit the holy grave in the Church of the Holy Sepulchre, the Church of Zion, the Cathedral of Saint James, and the Mount of Olives. They also visit the neighboring towns of Jerusalem, including Ein Karem—the home of John the Baptist, and Nazareth—the birthplace of the Holy Virgin Mary, and the Church of the Nativity, and they celebrate Holy Saturday and make a pilgrimage up the Via Dolorosa.*

Yoram rubs his eyebrows, once more experiencing the tangible burden of responsibility to protect the tourists. He feels confident that he will not let down the city which placed its trust in him and chose him to be the leader of the Jerusalem police force. He looks at himself in the mirror, inspecting his uniform as always, and marches out. He loudly orders several police officers to accompany him on a tour to inspect the three Locandas—Nathaniel, Dance Hall, and Vile—and to check on the safety of the foreign pilgrims. He wants to make a good impression on the tourists so that they have something to take back home with them of Israel and of Yoram.

The Prince of Peace

WALKING THROUGH THE CITY MARKETS with Rabab, I observe him taking his usual evening stroll with all his followers. The sky is clear and the stars flash like sequins on a woman's dress.

The king pays no attention to the women dispersed through the markets. I ask Rabab if she knows him and she responds that she doesn't, so I tell her, "This is Melchizedek, the Prince of Peace."

He strolls about the city, looking completely unconcerned. Rabab asks, "What age are we in now?"

"The age of the Jebusites. We're five thousand years away from your mother and father and sister Asmahan."

Rabab clings to my arm so as not to be carried away by the crashing tides of time. I tell her not to be afraid.

The peaceful prince walks into a bar at the end of the market and guzzles down a glass of wine as he fantasizes about the city of Jerusalem, which he so adores. Rabab and I watch him unnoticed, then walk back to our house, tired from our long walk.

~

A Morning Tour

SHE WAKES UP and gets out of bed, washes, and drinks her morning coffee. Then she dresses and leaves her house. (Ghazal has become a distant memory.) She moves humbly through the markets, as if she were going to or coming from a mosque or a church. She reverently touches the walls of the house, slowly inhales the smell of the stone, and carefully listens to the conversations coming from the balconies, conversations she believes only she can hear and understand.

She looks up at the welcoming windows, thrown open to the city wind, and feels herself once again sharing in the city's freshness and joy of life.

She looks at the people in the bars and by the open windows of their houses, and in the squares and on the stairs and there in the cafés and restaurants and here in the alleyways and there on the balconies.

In time, heavy with emotion, she returns home. In her personal studio, she pours out the things she's seen and a busy city forms on the blank canvas, weighed down with sorrow and loss.

The Description of the City

AT NIGHT, as I read the history of the city, I impulsively include Rabab in my reading. She's been standing by the window for a long time. I ask, "Do you feel like listening to what Nasir Khusraw said ten centuries ago about the city?"

"Read what he said. I can hear you from where I'm standing."

"I only enjoy reading with you when you're next to me."

So she nestles in close to me, and I read to her. "Jerusalem is a city set on a hill, and there is no water therein, except what falls as rain. The surrounding villages have springs of fresh water, but the Holy City has no such springs. The city is enclosed by strong walls of mortared stone, and with iron gates. Around the city there are no trees, for it is all built on a rock. Jerusalem is a very great city, the Holy City, and, at the time of my visit, there were in it twenty thousand men. It has high, well-built, and clean bazaars. All the streets are paved with slabs of stone, and wheresoever there was a hill or a ledge, the men of the city have cut it down and made it level, so that as soon as rain falls the whole place is washed clean. In the Holy City, there are numerous craftsmen, and each craft has a separate bazaar."

I look at her eyes to see if I should keep reading. She jumps up like a cat and takes off her nightgown, heading to the bathroom as she says, "I'm going to wash myself as this city washes itself in the rain."

I keep reading as I listen to the running water, like a river in flood, an uproar made song.

Those Days

SHE'S AT THE MOSQUE. She went to join a group of women and beg for forgiveness from God. At sixteen years old she loved a boy two years her senior. He reached for her breasts the moment they were alone in the storage room. She tried to push him away from her with shaking hands, strung with emotion, but she wasn't successful.

Her husband divorced her after their wedding night, and a loving father saved her from an otherwise surely harsh future. The neighborhood men told her he was scum. She lived at her father's house for three years before an even-tempered man came along who dabbled in many professions until he settled on being a fishmonger. He was ten years her senior, and he married her after his young wife died of a terminal illness.

There she is now, praying to her God, wondering why she can't let go of those days. She remembers them and feels confused.

~

The Darkness of the Night

THE ELECTRICITY goes out in the city, so Rabab and I stroll in the darkness of the night. She says she's afraid of the dark, so I grab her hand and walk close to her and say, "Don't be afraid."

She says, "Do you hear that? One of the daughters of Jerusalem is searching for her lover and grieving loudly. 'I opened for my beloved, but my beloved had turned away and was gone. My heart leaped up when he spoke. I sought him, but I could not find him; I called him but he gave me no answer. The watchmen who went about the city found me. They struck me, they wounded me; the keepers of the walls took my veil away from me. I charge you, O daughters of Jerusalem, if you find my beloved, that you tell him I am lovesick!'"

The lover's voice fades and we keep walking. I ask her, "Are you still afraid?"

"No. Disappear somewhere so I can look for you."

I stride away and hide in a nearby alley. She searches for and finds me. I hold her to my chest and in a whisper she asks me to take off her dress. So I do, and darkness blankets the alleyways and markets and neighborhoods and roads until sunrise.

A Scene

AS I WALK THE ROAD leading to al-Aqsa Mosque, in my mind I summon a dreadful scene: seven thousand people slaughtered by invaders' foreign swords, their blood running through the markets and squares up to a man's knee.

I walk and as I walk, I feel the blood drench my feet. I lift my right foot, then the left, becoming disoriented and beginning to sway as I walk, to the right, then to the left.

The scene haunts me. Blood floods the city's markets and squares, and it remains.

~

A Show

WE GO TO THE THEATER one evening. We leave the house and walk down Nablus Road by the graves of the sultans, then take a left and enter the courtyard of the National Theater, which holds so many men and women.

We watch a play about Jerusalem, which invaders have fought over throughout history. All of them have left, but the city remains.

The leading role is played by a talented woman with a sturdy body. At the end of the play, we cheer for her and for the other actors and actresses.

As we're walking home, she says she regrets not pursuing a career in acting. She claims a director came to her college when she was a student and announced he was looking to recruit actors and actresses. Many students answered his call, but Rabab hesitated.

She says the actress in the play touched her deeply and made her wish she could play her part or one similar so she could pour out all the energy bottled up inside her.

She speaks, and I listen quietly so as not to interrupt her thoughts. Every now and then, when she stops speaking, I squeeze her waist affectionately.

She halts and stands in front of me, blocking my path, and says, "It's not too late, is it?" I look into her eyes. She doesn't wait for an answer.

She runs to the house, and I run after her.

The Little One

SHE SAYS she heard him cry. He cried because his mother was asleep and he was looking for her breast. She says it upset her to hear the little one cry in her sleep. She wishes she were near him so she could pick him up, carry him in her arms, gently rock him back and forth to calm him, and stop his crying. She would give him her dry breasts to keep him quiet until his mother woke.

She says it was the little one crying that woke her. Abd el-Razzaq didn't hear any crying but he did wake up when she turned on the light. She tells him, "The baby is crying and his mother is fast asleep."

He asks her what baby she's talking about, but she doesn't answer him and goes on singing a lullaby. "Sleep, little baby, don't you cry." Abd el-Razzaq is confounded by what he's seeing and hearing, and Khadija continues singing to the baby so he'll go back to sleep.

∽

Photographs

I RETURN HOME with photographs in glass frames. The photographs were taken in the late nineteenth and early twentieth centuries.

There are photographs of shoeshiners at work and photographs of storytellers in Jerusalem cafés. There's a photograph of a man dancing with his dancing monkey, surrounded by a crowd of men and women. There's a photograph of female students at Jerusalem University standing outside their university with their teachers, a photograph of the Jaffa Gate, and another photograph of horseback riders and pedestrians entering through the gate.

When she sees me, she looks confused, as if she can't figure out what I've brought home this time. She won't relax until I show her the pictures, and then she declares that she loves black-and-white photographs!

We get busy hanging the framed photos. Rabab hangs the picture of the man and his dancing monkey in our bedroom, and she smiles mischievously as she does so. I want to hang the photograph of the college girls in that spot, but I don't tell that to Rabab out of respect for her wishes.

One Bullet

YORAM GOES UNDERCOVER, disguised as an Arabic-speaking foreigner. He wears the outfit of a resident of Jerusalem working in the wool trade and walks toward the Damascus Gate, expecting to find the horsemen. He's devised a plan that as soon as the army receives his phone call, it will immediately undertake a raid and take out every horseman.

Yoram is surprised to see the city stretch out vertically toward the sky. In a moment of agitation, he remembers that the city was destroyed seventeen times and now has been rebuilt for the eighteenth. Praise be to God, the city has once again risen from the dead, and Yoram will have to bear the heavy burden of responsibility for protecting all eighteen cities in one.

Yoram is overwhelmed by the responsibility assigned to him. He notices how the city up close looks like an eighteen-story building ascending into the sky, and sees peoples and merchants and vice presidents and brokers and tax collectors and investors and men of the cloth and scientists and intellectuals and hermits and smugglers and druggies and thieves and women in different fashions and armies marching out the gates of the city and others marching in and all the guards standing vigilant at these gates.

Yoram realizes he's not qualified to maintain and cannot guarantee the security of such a city. (It's later said that his marriage was on shaky grounds, too.) In a state of total despair, he takes out his gun and shoots himself. One shot.

He falls on the sidewalk, and the city keeps on living. It does not kill itself.

~

Besieged

I LEAVE THE OLD CITY in the evening and walk through the Damascus Gate toward my house. In my left hand, I carry bags of fruits and vegetables, and in my right, I hold the papers that haven't left my person for weeks and months. (I could be searched at any time.)

This evening Rabab and I are celebrating. I'm going to publish a book about the city, so we'll stay up celebrating until after midnight. Rabab will burn incense in our bedroom and she'll wear her silk nightgown, and I'll be plunged into the atmosphere of *One Thousand and One Nights*. The city is ready for us tonight—summer is a house without doors. I walk faster toward home, experiencing a yearning for Rabab stronger than any I've ever felt for her before. I hurry. The city walls look down on me suspiciously as night rapidly encompasses the buildings without asking permission. I reach my house but can't get in. Abd el-Rahman pops into my head and I wonder whether they've come for Rabab, or maybe, now, for both of us? Is it simply a routine search?

I wait outside. Rabab is home and by now she's probably wondering where I am. The soldiers have circled the house.

Friends

I SAY TO HER, "I've had many friends in my lifetime."
When she looks at me, I continue. "Some were per-
fectionists and those friendships didn't last long. They
couldn't forgive me my mistakes, sat on them like silent
demons. Some were very careful, and my heart experi-
enced so little pain that it turned as pale as a lemon.

"Others loved life, and they steered me away from
the drama that turns hair gray.

"Others were honest and trustworthy, but these
friendships didn't last long because death takes the good
ones first.

"And others were ugly in spirit. They would cheer-
fully smile at you in the morning and gnaw your flesh
come evening."

Here I am, talking to Rabab with her head on my
chest, about the mystery of how friendship takes root in
people's hearts.

~

Settlements

SHE ASKS ME with her head still on my chest, "Earlier you said that hatred can also take root inside people's hearts."

"I did."

She stands and walks toward the window to look out at the settlements surrounding the city on every side.

I rise, walk over to the window, and stand beside her. I bring my head near hers and we look out at the settlements together. There's no need to speak.

Birthday

MARY IS CELEBRATING HER BIRTHDAY. She invites Asmahan and Rabab to her party, so Rabab and I bring flowers and dessert and walk to the Christian Quarter. It's late afternoon and darkness creeps over the imprisoned city.

Rabab wears her silk dress, embroidered in red and green, and wraps a kaffiyeh around her neck. She carries herself through the city markets like a bride while I walk by her in my black pants and brown jacket. In the markets around us are traders and soldiers and movers and students and women from other times and places.

We kiss Mary's cheeks and wish her a long life. We shake her parents' hands and greet her old Aunt Janette. We sing "Happy Birthday" to Mary, and Mary and Asmahan and the girls dance joyfully in their white dresses, like a flock of doves. Rabab ties her kaffiyeh around her waist and dances an entire hour. Janette cries. She tries to hide her tears, but it's obvious. Maybe she remembers Mustafa and cries for him. Rabab cries, too, when she sees Janette cry. Maybe she cries because she remembers her parents' house, which they've been ordered to evacuate, or maybe she remembers her brothers, one in prison and the other somewhere in the world.

I cry as well. I cry because Rabab cries, and I cry because under occupation we have to be thieves and steal these moments of joy. I dry Rabab's tears and dance the last fifteen minutes with her.

Jerusalem, October 2009

Afterword

THE 155 VIGNETTES of *Jerusalem Stands Alone* (*Al-Quds waḥda-hâ hunâk*, 2010) build a narrative through moments. A girl comes of age. Her brother has disappeared somewhere in Europe. The narrator frequents a café and is detained by police. Laundry blows on the line. A faucet leaks. The daily routines of the characters unveil their relationships to each other and to their embattled city. As the narrative offers us bits of context, we come to understand the power of the unstated. Narrative gaps allow us to feel the emotional undercurrents that make this novel read like a sequence of prose poems—reveries on identity and place, family, and history.

Readers may be disoriented or liberated by the lyrical fragments. Mahmoud Shukair gives each character a distinct voice and story through deceptively simple, often haunting, language. We explore this vision of Jerusalem through characters who frequent real alleys, markets, and residences whose place names can be found on a map. The specific setting allows us to view Jerusalem through the eyes of people living there, their worries and small joys becoming ours.

Although the vignettes are loosely interwoven, they build on each other to form an intimate portrait of the inhabitants' lives. The bearded men, whose roles are never explicitly defined, are at first simply uncanny. Their beards are comedic but their demeanor is ominous, until at last their threat becomes visible when they mark the walls in red. They've come to claim Abd el-Razzaq's house. His family's helplessness and rage are unspoken but potent.

The ongoing pressure of history is shown more often than it is discussed. Yoram, the chief of police, reads a nineteenth-century document detailing tourist spots. Photographs from the same time hang on the narrator's wall. The pressure intensifies, until the narrator approaches the al-Aqsa Mosque:

> I walk and, as I walk, I feel the blood drench my feet. I lift my right foot, then the left, and feel disoriented and begin to sway as I walk, to the right, then to the left.
>
> The scene haunts me. Blood floods the city's markets and squares, and it remains.

What he senses is the 1099 assault on Jerusalem by crusaders. Contemporary accounts estimate seven thousand dead among the city's inhabitants, the streets flowing with blood. "And it remains."

Emotions are rarely named but when they are, as in "Settlements," silence quickly takes over:

> She asks me with her head still on my chest, "Earlier you said that hatred can also take root inside people's hearts."
>
> "I did."

She stands up and walks toward the window to look out at the settlements surrounding the city on every side.

I rise, walk over to the window, and stand beside her. I bring my head near hers and we look out at the settlements together. There's no need to speak.

Abd el-Razzaq's son, Abd el-Rahman, is arrested for being too quiet. It's funny and horrifying, but there's power in the unspoken. When the characters fall silent, Jerusalem speaks.

∽

Jerusalem Stands Alone provides insight into the full range of history of Jerusalem's long life. Below is a brief outline that may guide readers unfamiliar with the overlapping eras that underpin this novel.

Timeline of Jerusalem's Conquerors

Iron Age I (1200–1000 BCE)
Jerusalem is conquered by Canaanites (Jebusites)
Iron Age II (1000–529 BCE)
• 701 BCE: Assyrian ruler Sennacherib lays siege to Jerusalem
• 586 BCE: Babylonian forces destroy Jerusalem (Babylonian exile, ca. 597–539 BCE)
Persian Period (539–322 BCE)
Persian ruler Cyrus the Great conquers the Babylonian empire, including Jerusalem. Exiled Jewish people return.
Hellenistic Period (332–141 BCE)
Alexander the Great conquers Judea and Jerusalem. Ptolemaic and Seleucid rule.

Hasmonean Period (141 BCE–70 CE)

• 141 BCE: Hasmonean dynasty (indigenous) expels Seleucids

• 63 BCE: Roman general Pompey captures Jerusalem

Roman Period (70–324 CE)

• 70 CE: Roman forces destroy Jerusalem

• 135 CE: Jerusalem rebuilt as a Roman city

Byzantine Period (324–638 CE)

• 614 CE: Sasanian Persians capture Jerusalem

• 629 CE: Byzantine Christians recapture Jerusalem

First Muslim Period (638–1099 CE)

• 638 CE: Caliph Omar enters Jerusalem

• 661–750 CE: Jerusalem ruled under Umayyad dynasty

• 750–974 CE: Jerusalem ruled under Abassid dynasty

Crusader Period (1099–1187 CE)

Capture of Jerusalem

Ayyubid Period (1187–1259 CE)

• 1187 CE: Saladin captures Jerusalem from crusaders

• 1229–44 CE: Crusaders briefly recapture Jerusalem twice

Mamluk Period (1250–1516 CE)

Walls of Jerusalem dismantled

Ottoman Period (1516–1917 CE)

• 1340 CE: Tankiz dies

• 1517 CE: Ottoman Empire captures Jerusalem

• 1538–41 CE: Suleiman the Magnificent rebuilds the walls of Jerusalem

WWI to Present (1917–48 CE)

• 1917 CE: British capture Jerusalem during World War I

- 1947 CE: United Nations partition attempts to resolve Palestinian and Israeli claims.
- 1948 CE: State of Israel established. Jerusalem divided.
- 1967 CE: Israel captures Jerusalem's Old City and eastern half and illegally annexes East Jerusalem and a number of nearby villages in an effort to expand the municipal boundaries of Jerusalem. This annexation has not been recognized by the United Nations, the United States, or the international community.
- 2002 CE: Construction of the "security fence" begins

Note on Relocation

At the heart of the Israel/Palestine conflict is the question of who has a right to the land. The Israel State and Palestinian State claim the same territory. The 1947 United Nations partition attempted to resolve the two claims simultaneously but failed to result in a lasting settlement. The land dispute has recently focused on Israel's occupation of territories outside the 1948 boundaries—namely, the West Bank, Gaza Strip, and East Jerusalem. Israel withdrew from the Gaza Strip on September 12, 2005, but to this day continues to build Jewish settlements in Palestinian territories, actions deemed illegal by the United Nations (Resolutions 242 and 338) and other states.

Since 2002, the Israeli government has been building a security fence that winds deep into Palestinian territory, claiming the fence provides protection from Palestinian suicide bombers. The construction of new settlements and the security fence enables Israel to control important Palestinian economic areas, agricultural spaces, and natural resources. The International Court of Justice has ruled that Israel's West Bank barrier violates international law, but the unequal struggle over Palestinian land continues. The Israel/Palestine conflict, deepened by the tragedies of the Holocaust and the dispossession and occupation of Palestine, shows little hope for a two-state solution.

Glossary

Abaya: A loose outer garment worn by women in some parts of the Middle East. It is long-sleeved, floor-length, and traditionally black. The abaya is worn over street clothes when a woman leaves her home and is designed to hide the curves of the body. It may be worn with other pieces of Islamic clothing, such as a scarf that covers the hair (hijab or *tarha*) and a veil that covers the face (niqab or *shayla*).

Daughters of Jerusalem: The phrase Rabab recites in "The Darkness of Night" is a pastiche based on the Song of Solomon 5:7–8 (King James edition).

Verse 7: "The watchmen that went about the city found me, they smote me, they wounded me; the keepers of the walls took away my veil from me."

Verse 8: "I charge you, O daughters of Jerusalem, if ye find my beloved, that ye tell him, that I am sick of love."

Hodja, or Molla Nasr al-Dîn: In Iran, Turkey, and the Arab world, a comic character in short, comic folkloric narratives.

Jebusites: A Canaanite tribe which, according to tradition, occupied Jerusalem before its conquest by Joshua (Genesis 10:15).

Jilbāb: The *jilbāb* is a cloak worn over the head cover (*khimaar*), with similar coverage to that afforded by an abaya. A *jilbāb* is made of thick, opaque material that falls to the feet and is loose enough to conceal the shape of a woman's body. Free of designs or decorations of any kind, the *jilbāb* opens from the front and the sleeves are narrow at the wrists.

Kaffiyeh: The black-and-white kaffiyeh as used today is a traditional Arab head covering originally used to protect the head from sun and dirt. The kaffiyeh became important as a symbol of Palestinian liberation through its use by Yasser Arafat, the chairman of the PLO (Palestine Liberation Organization) and Fatah (in Arabic, Harakat al-Tahrir al-Falastini, a Palestinian nationalist political party and the largest faction of the confederated multiparty PLO). Traditional black-and-white kaffiyehs are identified with Fatah while red-and-white kaffiyehs are identified with Hamas.

Melchizedek: In Jewish and Christian tradition, the prototype of a just king (Genesis 18–20 and passim).

Nasir Khusraw (1004–88 CE): Persian poet, philosopher, and Ismaili theologian. His travel memoir, the *Safarnâma*, includes a description of Jerusalem, written a generation before the first Crusade.

New Tenant, The (*Le nouveau locataire*) (1955 CE): A one-act play by Eugène Ionesco in which the new tenant finds that workmen inexplicably keep filling the apartment with absurd amounts of furniture.

Al-Niffari: Muhammad ibn 'Abd al-Jabbar ibn al-Hasan al-Niffari (d. 965 CE), author of *Kitâb al-Mawâqif*.

Oud (also spelled *oudh*): A perfume made from the resin of the agar tree. (The musical instrument, *oud*, is from a different stem.)

Salim Sarkis (1869–1926 CE): Journalist and editor of the Lebanese newspaper *Lisân al-Ḥâl* (1877–1999), founded by Khalil Sarkis.

Tankiz (d. 1340 CE): Sayf al-Din Tankiz ibn ʻAbdullah al-Husami al-Nasiri, viceroy of Syria, 1312–40 CE. Known for public works, architecture, and infrastructure in Damascus. Khan Tankiz, near the Bab Al-Qattanin (both built by Tankiz), was once the old cotton merchant's market. It now houses Al-Quds University's Center for Jerusalem Studies.

Mahmoud Shukair, a novelist, playwright, and short-story writer, was born in Jerusalem in 1941. His writing largely deals with the intricacies of daily life in Jerusalem, and the impact of political upheaval on the lives of Palestinian and Israeli families. He has published over forty-five works, including TV series, plays, and articles. His works have been translated into various languages, but this is his first novel to be translated into English.

Nicole Fares, a Lebanon native, translates works from and into Arabic, English, and French. Her translations have been published in various journals and magazines in the United States. She is a PhD candidate in Comparative Literature and Cultural Studies at the University of Arkansas, where she teaches world literature and gender and sexuality theory. Her first translated novel, *32* by Sahar Mandour, was published by Syracuse University Press in the spring of 2016.